Traveling on One Leg

Traveling on One Leg

HERTA MÜLLER

Translated from the German by
Valentina Glajar and André Lefevere

NORTHWESTERN UNIVERSITY PRESS
EVANSTON, ILLINOIS

Northwestern University Press
www.nupress.northwestern.edu

Originally published in German under the title *Reisende auf einem Bein*.
Copyright © 1992 by Rotbuch Verlag, Berlin. English translation copyright
© 1998 by Northwestern University Press. Published 1998 by arrangement
with Rotbuch Verlag, GmbH, Hamburg. All rights reserved.

Printed in the United States of America

10 9 8 7 6 5 4 3 2 1

ISBN 978-0-8101-2706-7

The Library of Congress has cataloged the original,
hardcover edition as follows:

Müller, Herta.
    [Reisende auf einem Bein. English]
    Traveling on one leg / Herta Müller ; translated from the German by
Valentina Glajar and André Lefevere.
        p. cm.
    "Hydra books"—T.p. verso.
    ISBN 0-8101-1641-3 (alk. paper)
    I. Glajar, Valentina. II. Lefevere, André. III. Title.
PT2673.U29234R4513 1998
833'.914—dc21   98-34200
                                                                CIP

one

THERE WERE SOLDIERS BETWEEN THE SMALL VILLAGES under the radar screens revolving in the sky. The other country's border had been here. Its steep shore reached halfway up into the sky. The undergrowth, the lilac had become the end of the other country for Irene.

Irene could see the end most clearly when she watched the water as it hit the shore and flowed away. It hit the shore briefly and then flowed away for a long time, far behind the heads that were swimming until it covered the sky.

This loose summer Irene felt for the first time that the water's flowing away, far out, was closer than the sand under her feet.

Irene saw the notice—"Danger Landslide"—at the foot of the stairs to the steep shore, where the earth crumbled. It stood there as it had all the other summers.

For the first time this loose summer the warning had more to do with Irene and less with the shore. The steep shore was as if built of crumbled earth and sand, built by soldiers so suction couldn't come into the country, into the heart of the country from anywhere.

The soldiers were drunk in the evening. They went up and then down again. The bottles clattered in the undergrowth. The soldiers stood there under the radar screens far away from the bowling alleys and the dancing summer dresses in the bars. They only saw the light in the water and watched its color change. They belonged to the other country's border.

The sky and the water were the same at night.

The sky glimmered restless to itself, with scattered stars, driven by ebb and flow. It remained black and still. And the water raged.

Long after the water had gone dark and the waves high, the sky was still gray until night came from below.

Irene had walked along the shore for two hours, as long as the music of the rock group could be heard from the small bar close to the village. Two hours every night.

They were meant to be walks.

The first evening Irene looked out at the sky and at the water. Then a bush moved, but not like the other bushes. It was not the wind.

A man stood behind the bush. He said in a voice that was louder than the water hitting the shore, but still as if he were whispering:

Look at me. Don't run away. I won't do anything to you. I don't want anything from you. I only want to see you.

Irene stood still.

The man rubbed his member. He panted. The sea didn't take his voice away.

Then his fingernails were dripping. Then his mouth was broken and his face soft and old. The water hit the shore. The man closed his eyes.

Irene turned her back to him. Irene was cold. She saw smoke rising at the end of the bay where the boats were.

The wind moved the bush. The man was gone. Irene didn't walk to the end of the bay. She didn't want to see anyone. Where the boats were, where smoke rose. No face now.

Then the days that had come had been bright and empty.

Irene lived all those days only for the evenings. The evenings tied the days together. The jugular beat, the pulse, and the temples. The evenings tied the days so tightly together it was almost enough to hold the whole summer in place.

The evenings had not been walks. Irene went by the hands of the clock.

Irene was on time.

The man was on time.

Every night the man stood behind the same bush. He was half-covered by the leaves. Irene came through the sand. He had already unbuttoned his pants. Irene stood still.

He didn't have to say anything anymore. Irene looked at him. He panted. He panted every night for the same amount of time. The sea didn't wash his voice away. Every night his mouth broke in the same way and his face became soft and old.

In the same way the water grew louder when he stopped. And the bush grew tame in the same way. Only the wind made it move. Every night.

Irene looked for this man during the day. And at night when he was already gone. She looked for him by the bars. And she never saw him. Or she saw him so often that she didn't recognize him because he was a different person on the streets and in the bars.

It could have been a love affair. But on those days, when it happened, between the nights, Irene could find only the word *habit*. She had a feeling of loss. As if she hadn't come to her senses then in the nakedness between sand and sky. How could love be on time.

Irene was looking for this man when she found Franz.

She had seen Franz in front of the little bar by the railway tracks. Franz was sitting on the ground next to the entrance. His head was leaning against the chair.

Franz had been lying more than sitting. The rock group played loudly. The music was deafening. Franz was drunk.

The drunk spoke with his eyes half-open and looked open-mouthed to the sky. The legs of the village children stood in front of his face. They were scratched by the undergrowth. The children were barefoot.

The drunk spoke German to the children. He also spoke to himself.

The children picked up on his loose, incomplete sentences. They leaned their heads against the bush in the other country's language. They looked around when they did this.

It was a closeness in two languages that didn't understand each other. A closeness to a foreigner. A closeness that was forbidden.

The children giggled, insecure. A little bit malicious, a little bit sad, because there were things they didn't understand yet. But they knew this foreigner paid for the beauty of their sea with his drunkenness.

Long freight trains would drive past the village once in a while. They rattled in the night and deafened the music.

Then mothers were calling. The children left the drunk to himself, to the ground, the chair, and the bush. They ran along the tracks into the village without turning around. It had become dark long ago.

The musicians packed their instruments into their small cases. Only the drums were left between the tables.

What about the foreigner, the drummer asked. He pointed at the drunk and pushed his hair out of his eyes with the drumstick. He put the drumsticks in his coat pocket and walked toward the exit.

Come, he told Irene. Come on, that's it.

And Irene walked straight across the bar.

And she didn't come.

Irene walked up to the drunken man.

Come, said Irene. Come on, stand up. You have to get out of here, the police will be here any minute. Do you hear me.

Irene put the drunk against the next tree. She pressed his legs against the trunk so he wouldn't collapse.

Goodness, said Irene.

She didn't come up to his shoulders because he was so tall and heavy when standing up.

Why do you do this.

The drunk didn't do anything. He swayed and swayed.

Where do you live, tell me where you live so I can take you there. His face was thin. He looked open-mouthed into Irene's eyes.

God, where do I live. In Marburg, he said.

Irene laughed and sighed. She held him at his belt because he was so heavy and he was swaying. And he was much younger than she. And his shoes were full of sand. And the streets were so crooked.

Let's go to Marburg, said Irene.

He struck out at the air.

No, not to Marburg.

Not to Marburg, said Irene. Let's go to the hotel. Where is your hotel.

There were big apartment buildings along the shore. Hotels with a view for foreigners. Windows with a view of the distance. Irene wasn't allowed there.

The drunken man found his hotel. He found the key. He

found the elevator. The night porter was on the phone. Irene read the number on the key ring and found his room. She turned on the light next to the door.

There was a book on the table: *The Devil in the Hills*.

The drunk pulled the window open. Irene put him down on one of the two beds.

Is your name Franz. The children called you that.

He didn't understand the meaning of the question. He didn't say anything. Gray eyes, teeth pressing against lips, the incisors' edge like a thin, white saw.

I'm drunk, but you speak German. You're not drunk, how come you speak German.

Irene walked to the window. She looked outside.

I'll tell you tomorrow.

Franz wasn't aware anymore. Not even of the fact that he slept and that his mouth was open and dry and his lips as rough as the crust of the sand on the shore.

Irene saw the curtains hanging to the floor. She stared outside at the surface that lay black between water and sky. Franz moved his hands in his sleep. Sleeping like this under the light, his face looked absent on the white bed.

Nostalgia overcame Irene. And it wasn't nostalgia. It was a condition of things that were not alive. The stones, the water. The freight trains, the doors, the elevator, things that were moving.

The biting tracks of night were on the black surface outside.

Irene felt by the wind in her face that the room was high up. The stars bored into her forehead. The water raged below.

No, said Irene out the window.

She went to the sink. She drank cold water out of her

6

hand. She turned the light off. Like Franz she lay down in her clothes on the other bed. She felt the room going out the window in narrow grooves. Out in the empty surface were the dark was even deeper.

Irene couldn't cry in the dark.

Irene disappeared into her sleep.

Until the day cut into her eyes.

Franz came naked out of the bathroom. A spot of light felt its way along the wall next to the bed. Franz sat down on the side of her bed.

Last night, he said.

How did you get here.

I don't remember much.

Neither do I, said Irene. I have applied for a passport to leave the country. It's my last summer. I'm waiting for the passport.

Franz nodded.

I dragged you, said Irene. You were heavy.

Franz caressed Irene's fingers.

This sea, said Franz.

He looked at the ceiling. Irene touched the spot of light next to the bed.

Franz pulled Irene's fingers out of the spot of light and kissed them. He looked at his empty, crumpled bed. Then out of the window with his head half-turned to the side. The sun was big.

What do people eat in the village.

Fish.

And in the morning.

Fish.

And the children.

Fish.

Irene felt her tears running down her temples and into her ears.

I want to wash up, that's better than crying. Yesterday is still sticking to me.

Franz lay down on her:

I want to sleep with you.

The spot of light turned, it glimmered. Then Irene's head snapped shut. Her eyes were closed. They bored tunnels for themselves inward, through her whole body. She felt Franz, his bones, as if they belonged to her.

The body was hot and found the proper words. The whole body thought along, reflected when Irene said something.

Afterward Irene and Franz were at the station. Franz was leaving for Marburg.

Irene had a piece of paper with his address in her pocket. And in her hand the drawing in the sand. And the poplar leaf Franz had put where Marburg was. And the stone Franz had put where Frankfurt was.

Irene refused to think about parting.

Then the train had left.

Irene had gone through the poplar alley into the village. In front of the house she had seen one of the children who were in the bar the night before. The wind was blowing. Bushes were moving next to Irene's legs.

Out of sight, Franz had said.

And Irene: Out of mind.

Nonsense, Franz had said.

Irene went to the post office. Irene bought a postcard with the bay on it.

Irene wrote:

I don't really want you to write me. Because then I would

answer you. But it's me who wants to write to you. There is a difference.

When do you think you'll come, Franz had asked.

Irene sent the card in advance. She let it fall into the mailbox to Marburg. She heard it hitting the bottom as if it shattered to pieces. The mailbox was empty.

The noise on the bottom of the mailbox had been the sound of worries. The worries that were Irene herself. Impatience and waiting for the passport.

The operator was eating fish.

A room with a view of the distance, Irene said loud.

The operator smiled. She pulled a pointed, white bone out of her mouth.

Then the sea raged. Irene walked far away along the shore.

Irene walked fast. She wanted to be on time.

She had missed two nights.

Irene stood in the sand. Only the wind moved the bush.

The man wasn't there.

The water hit under the boats. It pulled them with it and floated them back to the sand. The wood cracked.

Irene heard voices, giggling voices.

A poplar moved. It wasn't the wind. Behind the poplar stood the man, and he rubbed his member.

Three girls were sitting below him on the sand. They were eating fish. They were giggling.

two

YOU CLOSED YOUR EYES, THE PHOTOGRAPHER
had said. You looked so serious, think of something nice.

I can't, Irene said, I don't want to either.

He pressed the button.

You press your lips together.

Irene pressed her lips together so she wouldn't close her eyes.

You would smile if you could see yourself.

He pressed the button.

If you knew what it looks like behind my eyes.

Irene didn't finish the sentence. She didn't even finish thinking it.

He pressed the button.

You can open your eyes. You can't see what's behind the eyes. Not with me. Would you like people to see it.

I wouldn't mind. I don't care.

You wouldn't mind or you don't care.

You said you can't see it. Why should I make up my mind.

Because it bothers you, otherwise you wouldn't have said it.

You said it bothers me.

I would take a picture of you with your eyes closed.

He pressed the button.

That doesn't work. You want passport pictures. The passport office doesn't accept pictures with their eyes closed.

But you put on makeup, you can't deny that you want to look beautiful. That's good of course. That's fine with me. Or do you put on all the makeup so that nobody notices it.

I put on makeup because once I wanted to be beautiful, Irene had said. It stayed that way.

The makeup, you mean.

Did anyone die, he asked.

Irene shook her head.

Then it's love, he said. With older people it's death, with younger people it's love.

He pressed the button.

Then Irene had felt like holding the passport pictures in the rain, but she hadn't. She had walked under the roof of the first house entrance. She had taken a picture out of the envelope and looked at it.

A familiar person, but still not like her. And where it mattered, where it mattered to Irene, the eyes, the mouth, and the groove between nose and mouth belonged to a stranger. A stranger had slipped into Irene's face.

The unknown in Irene's face was the other Irene.

Irene had dreamed that she was packing her suitcase.

There were summer blouses all over the room.

The suitcase was full.

Irene packed some more summer blouses. It was hard to fold them because they were so light that they slid out of her hands.

Irene heard steps behind her.

The dictator entered the room.

He stepped on the summer blouses. To him they were like leaves under a tree.

He walked through the room as if he had a wide, open street in front of himself. He walked up to the suitcase.

It's colder there, said the dictator.

He turned up his collar.

He put both hands into his pockets.

In her purse Irene had carried the passport with the other Irene's picture around town.

Four mailmen came out of the post office into the street. Each of them through one of the four compartments of the revolving door. The mailmen stood at the edge of the sidewalk and talked loudly while the door was still turning.

Confined to one of the compartments, Irene entered the hall of the post office to the rhythm of the revolving door.

The hall was humming.

Irene wanted to call Franz. In her thoughts she had figured out a few short sentences. Not even in her thoughts had they sounded credible:

I can't wait to see you. I have often thought of you. I almost cannot believe it. Or just: I'm coming. And the day. Irene didn't know the time yet.

The operator had asked for Irene's passport. She had talked too loudly. She had shouted.

Irene had dictated the phone number to her.

The operator had shrugged her shoulders:

I don't understand you.

She had written the phone number on a piece of paper only after Irene had spoken as loudly as she had. She wrote slowly.

Wait, she said.

She checked a list with her fingertip.

Marburg, Irene said.

I don't understand a word.

Irene shouted. The operator shook her head:

It's not here. It's not on the list.

Irene looked at the operator's fingertips:

Close to Frankfurt.

It's not in the directory.

Please, Irene said.

It's not here. Look, there is Hamburg, Freiburg, Würzburg. Everything is here. Step aside. You are standing in my light.

The operator had closed Irene's passport with a snap. She had handed it back through the window. She had said you're keeping me from doing my job. She had looked at the woman standing behind Irene.

The operator had moved the fingertip that had checked the list back and forth in front of her eyes since Irene had been standing there:

I'm not blind. You are deaf.

Irene had walked toward the revolving door. She had entered one of the revolving door's compartments. A man with a gray fur cap was in the next compartment. He had knocked with his fingertip on the compartment's glass pane:

The other direction, he had said.

Irene had turned facing the other direction

The man had turned the revolving door. Irene had gone out into the street to the rhythm of his steps, which she hadn't been able to see.

three

MEN WALKED ONE BY ONE THROUGH THE METAL
detector into the airport departure hall. The man in uniform
moved another detector up and down. It beeped at the coat
pocket of a man in a suit. The man in the suit raised his hands
and turned around. He was holding his boarding pass in his
mouth.

Everyone was looking at him when he entered the departure hall. After he sat down he looked toward the metal detector. They were checking another man in a suit. The man cor-
rected his sitting posture as he watched.

A woman's voice said through the intercom that the airplane was ready for boarding.

Irene was wondering which one of the men she could sleep
with. The men were getting up one by one. She examined
them again in the light of this question. She saw something
repulsive in each of them, things she had not seen before.

The older men had dark career rings around their eyes.
Their faces had been firm for many years. That they had aged
in that state comforted Irene.

Irene saw an older man wearing a big gold ring on his little
finger. She imagined herself lying in bed and waiting for this

man. She saw the man undressing. Hanging his jacket on the back of a chair. The pants on the seat of the chair. The shirt over the jacket. Letting his underwear and his socks fall on the carpet under the chair because he was used to despising them. Approaching the bed and realizing he had forgotten to take off his glasses. Using this forgetfulness to pull his gold ring from his finger, and to put it down on the table next to his glasses.

Irene heard herself saying: The gold ring must be there when you do it.

The conveyor belt was humming empty. The suitcases were not coming yet. Irene looked through the glass pane at the land outside. Her head was heavy as if the clouds were too close. As if gray, crumpled clouds were passing through her head.

Irene suspected she had only made up the story with the man, the glasses, and the gold ring because of the presentiment, reaching down into her fingertips, that Franz's face would be behind the door. And that it would still not be there even when Irene stood very close in front of his lips.

Franz wasn't there. His face wasn't close to the exit.

There was a man next to the exit holding a sign in front of his chest. The sign said: Irene.

Irene looked down with the feeling that her name was too common, and that it wasn't meant for her.

And Irene wanted to let the woman who was expected take her time. She wanted to see her going up to that man. What she looked like.

Irene heard the conveyor belt humming. All the passengers had walked past her.

Irene tried to remember when it had first happened that she couldn't stand something. And if she had then suspected that it would happen again and again. And if she had thought about what she should do with herself if she couldn't stand it anymore.

Suddenly Irene remembered one of the sentences in the books. A sentence that she had carried along all these years and changed: "But I wasn't young anymore."

It was as it is so often, as usual, as always when something is over: there was a wish on the roof of her mouth. Irene didn't know what it was. She only knew that it was hiding something from her.

An aftertaste had shrouded her in.

Yes, it was as it usually is, as always when something is over: gray in gray images would pop up too late and blow into each other. A trace of them got stuck in Irene's larynx.

Irene saw a wide, empty area with white markers.

Two men wearing suits moved toward each other through the grass on a strangely divided lawn. The grass was yellow and blew away. The men walked slowly, unintentionally keeping in step with each other. They walked. They were not looking forward to their meeting. When they came closer they acted as if they did not see each other.

When the tips of their shoes stood facing each other, almost touching, they hugged, one man looking over the shoulder of the other into the empty void.

They stood there hugging. Motionless. It was like a small everyday gesture you don't notice anymore.

Irene recognized the one face turned toward her.

It was the face of the dictator that had expelled her from the other country.

The dictator raised his eyes briefly. He looked at Irene.

Irene backed away, still looking at him so as not to let the dictator's face out of her sight.

The further Irene backed away, the closer the dictator pulled the unknown man toward him.

The sign with her name came toward Irene. And the man behind the sign said:

You are Irene. The description doesn't fit. I'm glad we found each other. I'm Stefan. Franz couldn't come.

He kissed Irene.

She looked at him when he carried her suitcase.

Irene looked into Stefan's eyes; he turned his head away.

Irene knew these avoiding eyes from the other country. This avoiding.

The people had another person in their larynxes when they spoke in loud voices in the arrival hall. Irene was familiar with this other person in the larynx.

Since the strange persons carried familiar persons in their larynxes they were not just strangers. They were stranger than strangers.

Irene wanted to repeat Stefan's last sentence. He had disappeared. The movement of the lips disturbed her hearing. Copying was harder than inventing.

four

THE CURTAIN MOVED.

The curtain moved even though the window was closed and nobody came in through the door.

It was a white lace curtain that looked like the cheap curtains in the rooms where many things happen all at once.

This was an office high up above the trees at the end of the city. An office in the Admission Facility.

You know of course, said the official, that you are at the Federal Intelligence Service. This is not a secret.

Offices are the same everywhere, said Irene. And it doesn't say on your foreheads who you are. And you haven't asked anything yet.

His chair cracked.

Did you ever have anything to do with the secret service there before you emigrated.

I didn't, but they did. That makes a difference, said Irene.

The official wore a dark suit of the type Irene remembered from the other country. The color between brown and gray. Only a shadow had that color. Only shirts that belonged to shadows were that kind of white and blue.

Let me establish the differences. That's what I'm paid for.

Irene also remembered the position of the head, the face half in profile, looking down a little. The chin always close to one shoulder without touching it when he spoke.

The official put a form on the table. There were types of faces on it. And columns for clothes: sloppy, sporty, stylish, elegant, functional.

Irene named five names and described five persons.

The official sifted through them. Only a handful of ambiguous meetings were left. That was Irene's life for him: thirty years under four eyes.

What did he, with his piercing looks, know of cars parking noiselessly at the curbstone, of the echo of bridges in the city, of fingering leaves in the park. Of roaming dogs shaking with hunger and walking on stilts, mating next to trash cans and howling in the middle of the day. They had the color of his suit. They were shadows, too.

Fingernails. Earlobes, the official asked.

They didn't matter then.

Think about them.

The official moved his head. His face helped Irene. She looked at it. She described what she saw.

Stick to the wording on the form.

He rested his chin in his hands.

Expanding forehead, meaty hands, dressed like you, said Irene.

He checked the "functional" box.

Did you want to overthrow the government.

No.

Cars were rustling out of the city, far below.

There was no column that could have described me, Irene

thought. The gentleman on duty was wandering straight across the fields. That was an expression from the other country. It meant sticking to something without understanding it.

The sky had changed outside. A cloud passed across the cleft between curtain and curtain.

The official saw Irene to the door:

In case you're still on assignment, my intentions are honorable.

The curtain recoiled when his hand touched the doorknob.

The curtain didn't move when the door moved.

Half a day had passed. A whole afternoon.

The air was cool. Irene looked with small eyes into the city's neon lettering, into the flickering channels of crossroads, into the forlorn, short streets.

Irene laughed silently. She pressed her arms tightly against her ribs. She walked holding on to the outermost edge of her soles.

There was something else going on in her head. It could have been the opposite of what Irene happened to be doing, if only she had known what it was.

There was no room in the Admission Facility. Irene lived in the refugee hostel. It was on Flottenstraße. Flottenstraße was a dead-end street.

The railway embankment was on one side of the street, the barracks on the other.

The Flottenstraße had the firmness of big harbors, of iron bars that duplicate themselves in the reflection of the water.

Unused tracks lay rusting on the railway embankment. Knotty trees pushed branches down to the ground around their trunks. Barren high up and heavily covered with leaves at the bottom. They were neither trees nor bushes.

The barracks was a brick building. It had two stories. But it looked too tall anyway because of the red bricks. Half of it belonged to the police. The other half was a refugee hostel.

A bed, a table, a chair. A water kettle and an iron closet.

A crane and prefab concrete parts outside the window. They were rocking. The construction site closed in on the room as Irene drank her milk.

People didn't have any sound in their steps in Flottenstraße. And the color of the faces in Flottenstraße was the color of old pictures. The dark spots on the cheekbones looked pale even though they were dark, or precisely because they were so dark.

Clothes were alms in Flottenstraße. Scarves yawned between necks and shoulders.

Irene knew the cheap shoes in the supermarket boxes. She had seen men and women shoving each other away and digging through the boxes. And among them children trying to pull their mothers and fathers away. And crying.

Irene had seen men and women who had found the one shoe that fits. How they held it in one hand over their head. How they continued to dig with the other one in the heap of separated pairs.

And this distance persisted from one shoe to the other. It grew behind their backs. It closed in on the shoulders, too.

The distance was in the eyes, too. And also later, when the refugees weren't walking in Flottenstraße anymore. When they went to the post office, or talked too loudly on the phone from a rough neighborhood. And wrote signs of life on cards to another country.

A city subway train passed behind the barracks. The sky stood, vertical. It beat against the eyelashes. The stairways were surrounded by wooden walls, because of the construction work. They were smeared with graffiti and sagging at the edges.

The wind up on the platform. The wall underneath. The light was loud. And the suction was cold.

Irene looked down at the barracks once again. Up at the railway embankment and the disused tracks once again. Down at the wall once again.

It was a stage set for crimes.

A man in uniform walked along the platform holding a walkie-talkie. He examined the silence with his eyes. He spoke into the walkie-talkie. He held it very close to his mouth when he spoke. He walked steadily. He didn't feel the suction.

The man in uniform was the first character in the play.

And Irene was the second character even though she hesitated to include herself.

The name of the play was the name of the station: Wilhelmsruh.

A cloud was thin and broken. It came from the other part of the city. From the other state.

There were two border guards behind the wall. On the barren strip where the earth was no good. Not even for grass.

The border guards were talking to each other. They followed the cloud with their eyes.

They were characters in the play since they turned around and checked to see if other clouds were coming.

A clock was hanging above the platform. A green light burned where the tracks converged.

The sentence had been passed before the crime had been committed.

A pair kissed. The train rushed through the tunnel. The

pair kissed; they didn't touch each other with their hands. The pointed lips urging each other on.

The kisses were short. The eyes stayed open. The lips dry.

There wasn't any passion in the kisses. Not even the lightness of a game.

There was a crimp in the kisses.

The changing of trains was the transfer in the kisses. The waiting for the next train.

As the walking up and down to avoid standing was for Irene.

Concrete around the shoes. Around the hair cold air that couldn't stand still. It tore at the hair.

The tunnel's yellow tiles appeared in the cold fluttering between the lips every time the two faces separated.

You couldn't tell the two from the wagons and the air suction when the next train came.

There was a bench next to the newspaper stand. The light inside fell on the back of the bench. Women smiled naked on magazine covers. Irene saw the air shimmering like a scarf in front of their nipples.

Irene leaned her back against the stripes of light on the bench. She wrote a card:

Franz, I called you. One day in the morning, one day at noon, one day in the evening. What for. Stefan told me you weren't here. I called you at night, too. I arrived too early. Or too late. You got me together with Stefan. Your face changes when I think of you. I want to see you.

The child held out its hand.

The mother gave it chips.

The child held the chips in its hand, like pigeon food. It ate. The mother bought a box of matches at the stand.

The child followed the woman with the suitcase with its

eyes. Then the woman with the bunch of lilies. Then the woman in the fur coat.

The child ate and followed the old woman with its eyes. The child didn't notice the other passersby.

It bent forward to see the woman with the hat.

The child held out its hand.

The mother gave it chips.

With his eyes the child followed an old woman carrying a box. The mother rattled the matches in her coat pocket.

The matches in the mother's coat pocket and the chips in the child's mouth made the same noise.

The old woman had put the box next to her shoe. She looked the child straight in the eye. The child felt the woman was going to smile the next minute because her cheeks were turning soft.

The child stopped eating. It turned away.

The child turned away so fast that there was flight in the short movement.

There was amazement in the old woman's eyes. The matches in the mother's coat pocket were still.

The amazement was as clear as a question. It crawled over the old woman's face. The cheeks became hard when it got to the mouth. The eyes became small. It was hate now.

The moving staircase was humming. The ticket machine clicked. Coins fell out.

The subway rustled from afar.

You don't need to button your coat, said a voice. A man carrying a bunch of lilies. He nodded. He wasn't younger, older, taller, or shorter than the woman. He was one of the passersby the child hadn't noticed.

The tracks grew bright.

The train stopped. The suction pulled away from the platform to the ceiling. It consisted of the cold air of a faraway wilderness and the hot air of close, heavy machines.

The platform remained empty after the train had left.

There were chips where the child had been.

There was a silence, a silence like that between hand and knife just after the deed is done.

five

I TRAVEL A LOT, SAID STEFAN.

The saleswomen stood behind crowded stands.

From the outside the Gedächtniskirche looked like a cavern from the inside, the Memorial Church: crumbling stone, dark, and wet. Further down were the lights of the stands.

The stands were full of the same stuff.

And Franz, asked Irene.

The stone glittered from one earring to the other. Stefan's chin didn't move:

Not a lot. But still.

Then glass candleholders in all colors. A drop was hanging from each of them. It didn't want to fall. It was frozen and agonizingly beautiful.

It was like when you can't cry anymore.

Does Franz live alone.

Maybe.

The woman between the candleholders read a book when she wasn't smiling. Then a man came up to her and kissed her. She looked at the book when he kissed her. She finished reading that one last sentence. She closed the book.

Stefan only looked at the concrete:

I only know Franz through his sister. We were friends once. She never lives alone.

The man is going to replace the woman, Irene thought, when the woman had closed the book. The woman didn't leave. She touched her hair. She looked at the man.

Is Marburg far from here, Irene asked.

Stefan looked her straight in the eyes.

And Frankfurt.

What for, Stefan asked. Franz is away.

I don't want to go. I'm only asking.

Irene thought those two will not be able to sell the candleholders by Christmas. They will pack them in boxes and move on.

Christmas, Irene thought.

It was like draping cat gut over fir trees.

I have to go on a trip, said Stefan.

He kissed Irene on the cheek. She looked at his receding face. I'll get in touch with you when I get back.

In front of the Admission Facility there was a yellow sign with a camera on it, crossed out in red.

An apartment, said the person in charge. You can move in next week. It's a hassle. You were lucky, you know. It's not so easy.

He mentioned a street name. It didn't mean anything to Irene. And he also mentioned a part of the city. Irene had heard of that one. She didn't know where it was.

He mentioned many street names. And how to get to where the apartment was.

The subway and the bus, he said. You like to take the subway, don't you. You need to take the bus more often, you see things from the bus. You don't know the city yet. Was there a subway where you come from.

No.

That's what I thought, he said.

The diagonal wrinkle in the middle of his forehead became deeper. It looked like the felt where his hat was squashed a little. Now it was lying on the desk. The brim, as long as a finger, covered the edge of the table.

Or a taxi, he said, a taxi is best.

Yes, said Irene, I'll take a taxi.

And then you get in touch with the building manager, he said. He knows you're coming. Do you have a lot of luggage.

A suitcase, said Irene.

Furniture.

No.

Well, then you need to buy a bed soon.

He laughed:

Mankind's greatest discovery is the bed.

A woman in boots was sitting in the subway. A woman in sandals was standing next to her.

It is the soft sliding away of all the seasons, Irene thought.

There had to be some thought between bed and closet. An inner concept of the day.

Maybe the concept hangs together with sleep, Irene thought. The warmth of the skin. Maybe the color of the floors on which light falls. The cardinal points or the vicinity of a park. Maybe a highway. Or the vicinity of a bridge. Or a book.

I'll find out about this when I have my apartment.

You couldn't figure out the noises that came from the road. The road itself became noise.

Frost high up. A revolving hustle and bustle down below.

There were certain places in the city where the frost lingered. It never left these places. You couldn't recognize them before you set foot on them.

These places were not street corners, crossroads, or bridges.

They were spots you would associate with dirt.

These places were close to trees.

A woman was standing under a tree. She shouted: Leo. She turned her coat collar up. She put her hand on the trunk. The space between her thumb and her index finger was big on the bark of the tree. It was as if the woman always had this distance in her fingers.

The woman looked up into the branches, briefly. A dog came running toward her. The dog was breathing heavily.

Come on, honey, said the woman. And she breathed louder after this sentence.

The dog was as tired as the woman on the cold place under the tree.

Irene closed her eyes as she walked. She tripped over something and got scared.

There was nothing on the spot where Irene had tripped. It was neither higher nor lower than the street itself.

A police car rushed across the bridge. The siren threatened. And further down, between the barren trees, the wailing sounded as if the siren were feeling happy: blood was being shed somewhere in the city.

Where did you live before, the building manager asked.

In the refugee hostel.

Where are you from.

Irene gave the other country's name.

Who have you got there.

Irene named the dictator's name.

You don't hear good things about him, he said.

He walked through the courtyard ahead of her. Irene saw the barren elder bush and the grass. Irene saw the windows gleaming. They were closed. Curtains. A wheel of white paper was turning on one balcony. It squeaked at the stick. Irene heard it because the courtyard was so quiet.

How long have you been here.

Irene counted over the time since she came here. He sized Irene up. Starting with her shoes. And when he said something he didn't think about the sentences coming out of his mouth. He talked and asked as if all that was meant just to look at and let be. And he tried to figure out whom he had there.

Thoughts came to Irene's head and left again. And none had anything to do with her. Her suitcase stood next to the staircase casting a shadow next to the door. And no thought urged Irene to stay. And no thought urged her to go.

The building manager had pressed the key to the garbage in Irene's hand.

Irene carried her suitcase upstairs through the staircase.

As she walked into the apartment, a hallway walked through her. Then a kitchen. Then a bathroom. Then a room. Nothing but empty walls. Irene only noticed later that there was a stove in the kitchen. And only after the building manager had left did she notice a pickling jar with salt in it on the stove.

The suitcase stood closed in the hallway for a long time as if Irene were only half-alive. She couldn't think or walk. She tried to speak to see if she could still do it. She didn't know if she really said something.

Irene looked along the wall for a place for the bed.

I'm a waverer, said a deep voice.

Who are you, asked Irene.

Waverer.

You have the wrong number.

The voice laughed, and it was Franz's voice.

A waverer, don't you know this word.

Not exactly, said Irene.

Neither do I, said Franz. I was at the university yesterday, I had to turn in a paper. I tried several excuses on the way to the university. Acted them out. They weren't excuses. I wanted to lie. But then, in front of the professor, I forgot which lie was the better one. And before I could open my mouth, the professor looked at me and said: You procrastinate for so long until you don't know anymore what you wanted to write in the first place. You are a waverer.

The clock was ticking. The dial was dusty.

I want to visit you. I don't know when yet, said Franz.

Waverer, said Irene, a rare word. It makes you think of wayward, but without a will.

You know, said Irene, your voice is different than the one in the other country. It's different even when you don't disguise it.

I hear myself when I speak. I couldn't hear myself before. I speak in my ear or I speak through the ears, said Franz.

A child lay down on a wide bed. It crossed its legs. Put its arms under its head.

The child closed its eyes and laughed.

Sleeping and laughing don't go together. You'll get a large bed when you grow up.

She held the child's shoes by their shoelaces. She let them swing:

You'd get lost in it now. It's even bigger at night, my love.

The child looked at her. Then it closed its eyes.

She is afraid at night, said the woman, she was even in her crib. Then she comes crawling to us.

She smiled as if she wanted to say more.

The child opened its eyes. It yawned:

Say good morning.

The child looked at Irene's mouth. It shouted:

Say good morning.

You haven't slept, said Irene. It isn't morning.

I can say good afternoon if you want me to.

The woman pulled the child's legs toward her:

You can't see the bed because of us.

She put the shoes on the child.

It's too big even for me, said Irene.

The woman tied the laces without looking:

A king-size bed. If you sleep alone it makes no sense. She put the child on the floor.

I've seen narrow beds on the other side.

A strand fell, hesitant, across the woman's ear as she bent down. It fanned out, across her cheek, across her mouth.

Irene felt the blood beating in her wrists. She saw the official's dry tongue again like a pale, half-covered leaf on the flowery cover of the wide mattress.

I actually want a bed for the guest room.

The sky over the courtyard disappeared this night, too. Even the grass disappeared.

The walls disappeared, too, since they were as black as the sky and the grass.

A rectangle was shining.

Considering its length it could be a door. But because it was shining high up, Irene knew it was a window.

There was a room behind the rectangle. A second man showed up every night behind the man in the T-shirt. This one put on a coat. Shortly afterward, a woman would enter the room every night. She would take off her blouse.

The man in the T-shirt would disappear every night. And the man in the coat would disappear every night.

The woman without the blouse stayed. She would talk.

Every night there had to be another person in the room.

One Irene couldn't see.

That person must have been the reason why the rectangle was shining at night.

Irene was afraid to undress because the light outside was so gray. She was sitting on the edge of the bed. She took off her shoes. Irene lay down in her clothes. She saw her shoes standing in front of the bed.

Irene covered herself.

It was hard to keep her eyes closed.

The eyelids were too short. Light was coming through the eyelashes. The gap of light under the eyelids was so glaring as if the light in the room came from below. As if the floor was shining into her eyes.

Irene turned her face to the wall.

You could clearly see a rectangle on the wall. It was whiter than the rest of the wall. The rectangle was not as white as lime. It was white as skin. It was a back.

Irene saw the ribs through the skin. The back was breathing. It was also warmer than the rest of the wall. Irene thought of Franz.

Irene felt the warmth of the back, the warmth of the bed, the warmth of the clothes, and the warmth of the skin.

Each warmth was different.

The edge of the blanket lay around her neck. Irene felt as if she was buried.

Her eyelids grew longer. They were enough for the whole face. Irene's eyelids were enough for the whole room.

They slowly closed.

They turned into stripes of shadow like blinds.

six

THE FLOOR IN IRENE'S ROOM WAS PAINTED DARK brown. It took the light away from the ceiling and the walls. It had the same color as the walls of the courtyard.

What kind of people were they, said Stefan.

Irene shrugged her shoulders. She didn't know the former tenants.

Stefan knew two Poles.

It takes two or three days, said Stefan. It's work done on the side, as you know.

The two Poles came very early in the morning. They brought two traveling bags. They took the power sanders out of the traveling bags. They put them next to the wall. They took off their shoes.

One of the men looked into the courtyard and shook his head. The other one checked the floor with his fingertips.

Keys, said the man standing at the window.

Faces from the East, Irene thought. She recognized this kind of tiredness that had nothing to do with work or with rest.

Where are you from, Irene asked.

Poland, said the man at the window.

What place.

The man named the name of the place. Irene didn't understand what he said. She nodded.

A lot of dust, said the man who had checked the floor.

Irene wrapped the phone and the clock in plastic bags.

I'll be back in the evening, said Irene.

The man at the window saw Irene to the door. He walked in his socks on the tips of his toes. He locked the door from the inside and put the chain on. You could hear the power sanders buzzing all over the courtyard.

The two Poles were gone when Irene came in. The sanders were wrapped in the traveling bags. They stood behind the door. The Poles had sanded off two spots as big as four tabletops. There were empty juice and mineral water bottles along the wall. Half-smoked cigarette butts were in the ashtray. They smelled like cigarettes from the other country.

The two Poles came and left in the dark for three days in a row. For three days they took off their shoes and walked through the apartment in their socks, on the tips of their toes. For three days the sanders buzzed in the elder bush and the grass when Irene walked through the courtyard. And in all the windows of all the walls.

There were more empty bottles along the wall every night.

The tiredness that Irene knew from the other country remained the same on each of the three days. Irene knew it was in all the pores. The tiredness was danger. The fear of the sander's noise filled each pore of the two faces.

Nothing changed during those three days. Only the sanded spots on the floor grew larger and larger. On the third night they were as big as the room.

Irene bought a postcard. There was a swimming pool on the card. Black and white. The heads on the water were gray.

There was a chessboard with pieces on it next to the swimming pool. The water moved under the chessboard. The chess players were standing in the water. They were thinking. They looked straight into the picture. The postcard was a chess players' postcard. They were the object of the picture.

A man was sitting to the side. He was holding his chin in his hands. He was looking at the water. The photographer must not have noticed him when he took the chess players' picture. The man sitting to the side didn't belong in the picture.

For Irene the chess players' postcard was the postcard of the man sitting to the side. Only this way did the postcard become unfinished.

Something had been happening to the man sitting to the side since Irene bought it two days before. It seemed that more than two days had passed for him.

Irene cut off the edge of the pool where the man was sitting. The scissors didn't touch the chessboard.

The man lay crooked on the water. Irene also cut the water away. The man fell into Irene's hand.

I almost drowned him because he wasn't indifferent to me, Irene wrote on a sheet. He couldn't bear the swimming pool as you couldn't bear the sea.

Franz, I hesitate while I'm writing you. There is this longing that makes people lethargic. My hand is almost going to sleep now while I'm writing to you.

Irene folded the paper and slipped the man inside. He was lying as if lying in the snow. It was too late for him. It was like afterward.

Irene wrote Marburg on an envelope. With capital letters as if that were enough. Then Franz's address.

Irene was confused when she stood before the mailbox. Under the slot it said: Other Directions. Other Directions was as big on the mailbox as Marburg on the envelope.

The postcard with the swimming pool on it lay on the kitchen table. Irene slipped her hand under the spot where the man had been sitting. She could see her fingernail.

Had Irene not taken the postcard with the swimming pool on it from the kitchen into the living room, it would have become the story of a fingernail lying to the side.

The postcard was lying next to a man you could only see from behind, next to a fish.

The railing of a high street next to a man carrying a white glove through the park. An old man reading the newspaper on a bench under the empty sky next to a church tower. A big thumbnail next to a driving bus. A watch next to a gate thrown open and the cobbled pavement in front of it led to emptiness. A Ferris wheel with flying people next to faraway water. An airplane in the sky next to a hand. A face flying at high speed next to a girl in a rocking chair. A hand pulling the trigger next to a man driving a bike through the reflection of the trees. A screaming mouth that reached up to the eyes. Two men with peaked caps standing and looking at the water. An old woman sitting on a balcony above the city. A woman with black sunglasses. A corpse in a suit. A water mill. A room turned upside down. A boy in a sailor suit. A shopping street. A revolving door in the Rocky Mountains.

Irene cut out newspaper pictures. She rarely cut the edges straight. Which meant they were rarely black. The edge looked as if the newspaper was about to take the picture back into the paper where Irene's hand trembled.

Irene glued the pictures next to each other on a sheet of wrapping paper. She had to look and compare for a long time until two pictures fit together. Once they fit they fit automatically.

The connections that appeared were opposites. They made one single, strange collage out of all the pictures. The collage was so strange that it could relate to everything. It was constantly moving.

The collage was so strange that it reached the point where the smile of the girl in the rocking chair unveiled the same abyss as the corpse in its suit.

Irene hung the picture on the kitchen wall. She was sitting at the kitchen table. Her looks were steps.

Irene looked for a main character in her collage.

The main character was an object: the gate thrown open and the cobbled pavement in front of it that led into emptiness.

The kitchen table stood on the cobbled pavement. Irene held the knife and the fork as the old man held the newspaper in his hand under the empty sky.

The cutting, chewing, and swallowing barely passed through Irene's thoughts. They touched Irene's mouth so briefly she didn't know what it was.

The revolving door stood still. It stared into her plate from the Rocky Mountains.

There was only one picture left. It didn't fit into the collage.

It was a picture of a young man. He had a dark forehead, shining eyes. He held his hand on his chest so you could see the moons at the roots of his nails. His lips were half-open.

The man was a politician. He had lost his power. Shortly afterward he had been found in a luxury hotel at a lakeshore.

The politician was young and dead. Murder or suicide, nobody knew.

These days the politicians on the TV screen were stranger than ever. They looked for each other and were distressed. They sat around edges of tables like dragonflies on the edge of a boat.

The tables were rocking. The politicians showed consternation. But their foreheads were dark with power. Their eyes were shining with despair. And hypocrisy made the roots of their nails more and more white.

The picture of the dead politician lay alone on the floor in Irene's room for half a day.

Irene combed her hair. She saw the picture in the mirror. Irene put the picture face down, still holding the comb in her hand.

Irene closed the front door. She buttoned her coat as she walked. Her steps sounded double on the stairs.

The cold came from inside. The coat's collar drove it to her throat. Irene's hair was freezing. Her scalp ached.

Once in the courtyard she looked back up at the windows one more time. She felt damp cool spots under her arms. She was sweating.

Then Irene was standing in front of the apartment door again.

She ran into the room. She put the picture into her coat pocket. Irene saw the key ring still swinging in the keyhole when she went back to the door.

There was a tired light above the street.

A woman said: It's going to snow today. I feel it in my legs. Irene had never seen the woman on this street before. She was old. Carrying a polished walking stick. You could tell from her coat how much it cost.

Irene crossed the street next to a mountain of cut branches. They were not from any of the trees in the street. They had been lying in the same spot for several days. They hadn't changed. The leaves stayed green because it was cold. They broke when you touched them.

Irene reached into her coat pocket and crumpled up the picture. She let it fall into the wastepaper basket.

Then Irene was captured by the feeling that everything could suddenly change in the city. The old women with their white perms, polished walking sticks, and healthy shoes would suddenly be young again and march in the League of German Girls. Long, windowless cars would drive up to the doors of stores. Men in uniform would confiscate the merchandise on the shelves. And in the newspapers laws would appear like those in the other country.

A woman was leaning against a phone booth. Chewing gum. Looking down the street with empty eyes. Blowing white bubbles out of her mouth. They burst in the air. White shreds stuck to her lips.

A car parked at the curbstone. The woman pushed herself away from the phone booth. She ran toward the man. She welcomed him with a milk-white bubble in her mouth.

Irene went into the subway station. There was a photo booth there.

Irene drew the curtain. She let a coin fall into the slot. She looked in the mirror. She pulled up her blouse and looked at her breasts in the mirror. Then Irene combed her hair. Hair forward, hair backward. One ear covered, the other ear naked. Then Irene blew back the hair from her forehead.

And Irene cried because the hair flew that way and because a part split in two like a white piece of thread on the middle of her scalp. And the light flashed. And the subway rustled and stopped.

Irene waited for the pictures in front of the machine. The subway had left. The air crackled in the station.

Irene knew there was a man inside the machine. Because the picture was warm. It was body heat.

And there was an unknown person on these pictures, too, like in the other country, like on the passport pictures.

The other Irene was also on the pictures out of the photomat.

seven

YOU'VE BEEN HERE FOR A WHILE NOW, SAID THE official.

The word *while* lay still on his face like the shadow under his chin.

Are you homesick.

Irene saw his eyes moving as if they didn't have enough room under the eyelids.

No.

Don't you ever think back.

Very often.

And then.

You said homesick.

Irene looked for a spot on his coat, something for her eyes to hold on to.

You are so sensitive, said the official, so sensitive. As if our country has to make up for everything your country did wrong.

Irene's eyes stuck to a button.

We all have our own plans, said the official.

Our life story, said Irene.

No, our plans. A life story cannot be wrong.

Irene said as if to herself:

I only know life stories that are wrong.

The official opened his mouth. He didn't say anything. His tongue stood in his mouth as if it didn't have enough room. As if there had been something else under it. Something that was not a tongue. As if there had been a finger under his tongue. A dry finger in the middle of his mouth. Irene put the money for clothes into her purse.

In the secondhand stores the clothes were divided into fields. Columns of shirts, jackets, and pants.

The air from the fan grabbed at Irene's face.

Monotonous Muzak was droning on in the room. Obsessive like an endless sliding down on iron bars.

Irene had often heard the word *scene*.

Years hit the woman in the face as she tried on the green coat and looked into the mirror. A stone was glittering in one nostril. Her red hair had shades of pink in it and holes so deep that her scalp looked like a wound.

The coats were hanging in the back room. The metal buttons and the buckles were covered by verdigris. The coats had survived wars. Irene didn't touch them. Coat hangers like shoulders.

The cloth was stiff. It had covered skin for many years. It had rushed people onto the city streets. It had eaten dust. It had witnessed hard work, smoking, and drinking. It had hung in corners. It had lain next to beds. It smelled of poverty and love on the run. The cloth.

The price tag rubbed against the pink-and-red-haired woman's neck. It looked like a military postcard.

The woman paid for the green coat. She tore off the military postcard. She put on the coat. She went out into the street.

43

She walked very fast. Faster and faster. She began to run. Down the stairs into the shoe store. She didn't take the escalator.

There was more anxiety than hurry in her small steps.

There was the anxiety of a watchful exposure to danger in everything the woman in the green coat did.

She walked along the mirrors. There were shoes in the dull strips. The woman's eyes walked in the mirror's strips. The ends of her hair. Her neck.

Above the woman's hair it said: Great strides for small feet.

The woman took a shoe from the shelf. She weighed it in her hand. She looked at the sole. She put the shoe back. She weighed a second shoe and a third shoe in her hand and looked at their soles. She put the shoes back.

The weight of the shoes was the price. It was on the sole.

Music circled around the shoe store. It became louder when Irene stood next to the shelf.

Irene didn't move so as not to escape from the monotony of the rhythms.

The woman had weighed and turned the fifth shoe in her hand. She didn't put it back. The woman took off her own shoe, the one she had brought from the street.

The woman's stocking had a big hole at her big toe. She bent the toe as if she were hiding her finger. She was looking for a look in the mirror's strip. She wasn't looking for her own look or for Irene's. She was looking for the saleswoman's look. She who was at home in the store. She who knew the measure of all things. The measure of shoes and the measure of prices.

The saleswoman knew the measure of the women coming into the store and exposing their stockings in front of her.

The saleswoman put more shoes next to each other than fit the length of the shelf.

The same shoes Irene was wearing were standing on the shelf.

The music sounded tired. It was hanging in the room like sultry air. As if the text couldn't stand the tune.

The saleswoman blew dust from the shoes.

The woman with the pinkish-red hair had left. Gone out on the streets, to the city.

Irene walked toward the door. She walked slowly, so as not to be noticed. She didn't want to leave. She wanted to disappear as the woman had disappeared.

Irene was waiting for the saleswoman's voice.

You've stolen these, the voice would say. And point at Irene's shoes.

Irene was sweating. She knew she wouldn't deny this sentence.

She wouldn't deny the accusation. She wouldn't say anything.

She would believe the saleswoman. She would remember that she had left home in her stockings. That the sidewalk had been wet and full of sand. That cigarette butts had stuck to her stockings for a couple of steps. Irene began to run.

Small stones, speckled green and black, trickled down onto the asphalt. They bounced back like hail. They ran here and there.

Irene's necklace was broken.

She bent down. She felt small stones running down her back as if her spine were going to disintegrate.

She straightened up. She looked up along the wall of the store. There were balconies above the store windows.

Two men went by. Talking to each other. They didn't step on the small stones.

It had snowed all night long, said one of them. In the morning we wrote our names on the slope.

Love in winter, said the other one.

Irene listened to the sentences. The two backs went away. People walked by fast. Without thoughts of their own. They stayed close to the backs to follow the conversation.

The cars that drove by sprayed the wet air. It was cool on the cheeks.

The two backs were small with distance. They moved closer together. A bike passed by them.

One of the necklace's small stones was tardy. Only now did it fall on Irene's shoe.

Irene walked in the direction away from the two backs. She walked out of the conversation. She made an effort not to listen to the sentences spoken by the passersby. She listened to the cars driving by. They rocked before they stopped when the light was red.

Irene touched a fur coat's sleeve. It was soft as if it breathed.

Irene walked under a red umbrella, the time it took to take two steps.

What region were the two backs talking about, Irene asked out loud. What slope.

The boy on the other side of the street was wearing an old leather jacket. He was also talking with his hands.

The girl was carrying a schoolbag. She was quiet. She nodded. When they got to a gate, the girl went into a dirty courtyard without saying good-bye.

The boy stood in front of the open gate and followed her with his eyes.

No one will be happy who can only leave this courtyard with a bridegroom or who pulls himself a bride out of this corner.

eight

FRANZ WAS OVER FOR A VISIT.

The pillow next to Irene was empty. The sheets crumpled.

Franz was already up. He had made noises that fit in with Irene's dreams.

Irene only woke up when Franz was standing at the window, not making any noise.

The closet was shining. The wood was so bright that it needed a little bit of shadow.

Franz looked into the courtyard. The rug's design ran slowly under the table. The tablecloth moved.

Franz squashed dry leaves in his hand. He tore yellow leaves from the houseplant's branches. Dust whirled behind his back. Or was it the sun in the room.

Now I know, said Franz, what I miss in your apartment. I miss the street under the window.

Irene's answer was stuck in her throat until her eyes reached the grass in the courtyard. The grass was against her and the elder bush was against her. Even the salt line on the walls.

This is getting on my nerves, said Franz. A house without a street.

Irene searched the clothesline with her eyes. It was empty and it moved.

I know, said Irene, there is no peace in this yard, there is only silence.

Franz put the yellow leaves on the windowsill:

Yes, and it is because I'm not at peace that I cannot stand this silence. You don't know what I mean. You have good nerves.

Irene wanted to go to the table instead of saying something. She couldn't take the steps because Franz was looking at her, quietly.

Irene leaned back slowly as if the closet weren't allowed to feel her:

There's nothing I can do about it.

In the evening Irene went out on the street.

A cigarette was gleaming on the sidewalk as if someone had disappeared on that spot.

Irene thought with her next breath: Franz will never come back again.

There was only white in the eyes of the passersby. The pupils had stolen away into the darkness. The faces, parts of the faces, were in the light, the faces couldn't stand it.

The parts of the faces in the light looked like shadows because of the darkness.

The leaves of the tree were the backs of leaves. The trees were the backs of trees. The whole city was the back of a city.

There was a man on the corner. The sleeves of his coat were too short. His wrists were too thick. He was carrying a briefcase. It was flat and light.

The man whispered as Irene walked by. His voice was soft. His eyes were shining. His look was cold. The man disappeared in the restroom. Irene heard him talking behind the door.

She closed her fingers tight around the apartment key in her coat pocket. A puddle shimmered, ruffled by the wind. Irene saw the man's member standing erect, reflected in the puddle. And the water was rocking back and forth.

The cracking of a dry branch under a shoe had the unpredictability of an attack.

Irene had never seen a customer in the curtain store yet. A lamp was shining next to brown velvet.

A white plastic bag was lying on the road. A passing car scared it away. It fell to the ground. It didn't turn over.

Irene heard three identical notes on the other side of the street. Short, identical whistles. And steps in between. She saw the briefcase.

The man didn't know the game in the puddle where the water rocked itself back and forth. His lust wasn't satisfied. Or was it. Satisfied lust.

If so, his newfound equilibrium drove him further into the night. It was an equilibrium that required fear.

The man's whistling was like walking over bodies and singing.

Then Irene stopped in front of a bar.

Irene was overcome with helplessness when she entered a bar alone like now. As soon as she had sat down at a table she asked herself why she had come. Not to eat, not to drink, not to talk. Maybe to walk into a room from the street.

The wood and the wall and the looks filled the air when Irene wanted to breathe. Everything turned itself upside down.

The faces shared the watching and the drinking with Irene.

Irene sometimes wished to share something with these looks. But she didn't know if she really wanted it. And what there was to be shared. The sense of sharing was noncommittal.

The participation halfhearted and slow. It made little sense to put up with it. And it made little sense to flee from it. Maybe bearing it was the word for what Irene did.

Irene's hands would often tremble when she sat alone at the table and reached for the coffee cup. Her eyes would often close. The bottles on the shelves seemed to swim when Irene looked at the bar.

The waitress's face seemed to grow older as Irene looked at it.

I believe I'm very old, Irene had said one evening to Stefan in this bar. I have believed it for twenty years. When I was ten I often wondered how you can pass the time until you're twenty.

Too old, Stefan had said.

No. Very old, not too old. I don't feel too old.

Were you also born yesterday, asked the man at the bar. I like you.

A hair was hanging from the man's lower lip.

Born yesterday. I mean I wasn't home last night.

The hair on his lower lip was not his hair. Very dark and supple. He didn't feel it.

I have no homeland. I'm Italian. Born in Switzerland. A second-generation foreigner.

I have a homeland. It's just that I'm abroad.

A foreigner in a foreign country.

He laughed. Just abroad.

My children will be the third generation.

Will be.

Are.

How many, asked Irene.

The third.

How many children.

Three. My wife.

Your wife.

No, she is German. She doesn't understand.

That you have no homeland.

Maybe.

That you were born yesterday.

The hair was hanging into the glass.

And you. He took Irene's hand.

The hair moved off over the edge of the glass.

Generations, said Irene. Sometimes I try to think of someone and I can't do it. She thought of Franz.

You have to like a man in order to pluck a hair from his mouth, Irene thought. You must have thought of him a lot, and time must have passed.

She didn't want to think of anything else as far as this man was concerned. Next thing he'll ask what I'm thinking about. I'll say: Nothing.

The man didn't ask that.

Yes or no, he asked.

He had spoken many sentences. Irene didn't know what this was about. She saw that his face was bloated.

You are right, said Irene.

That's what all women say. And afterward I'm alone.

The man laughed with several voices at once.

Irene shook her head.

So it's no, he said.

He nodded

Maybe you'll think of me, he said.

Irene walked to the next mailbox.

She took a postcard out of her pocket and wrote: You know, sometimes I'd like you to be closer than a store window, or a branch, or a bridge. But even while I think about this I realize how I keep losing sight of you.

As she was writing the postcard, sentences came to Irene's mind that she didn't carry in her head. She didn't have them on the tip of her tongue when it was between her and the streets.

Whenever she tried to relate to Franz and to herself, everything outside Irene suddenly had properties.

The asphalt was referred to as length and width. If the asphalt had a personality of its own it could bring the city to a halt. The city would then be just a sidewalk, a wall, or a bridge.

The city would be dammed up if the asphalt had a personality. That gave Irene a sense of outer safety.

But her own inner insecurity was uncovered, washed up in Irene's head. You couldn't dam that up.

The city and her skull were an alternation of movement and immobility.

The asphalt grew larger when the skull stood still. The emptiness in the skull grew larger when the asphalt stood still.

Sometimes the city attacked Irene's thoughts. Sometimes Irene's thoughts attacked the city.

Irene crossed the street on red.

A man caught up with her. He was smoking. He walked with slow steps.

Irene wanted to let the man overtake her. He didn't overtake her.

The smoke passed over her face. Irene turned her face away. She heard the man's breathing. And that he walked in step with her. She changed her step.

She only looked at the walls of the houses now. She felt that the man moved his arms to the same rhythm as she did. She didn't move her arms anymore.

It was dark. The feeling of not having arms made Irene dizzy.

It's like lying in bed and pretending to be asleep, Irene thought. And it's like forcing something out of fear.

A few more steps, Irene thought, and the man will have the feeling that I belong to him.

Irene walked around the corner so she wouldn't belong to the man.

nine

IRENE HAD MET THOMAS THROUGH STEFAN. ON
the banks of the Landwehrkanal. The sun had been warm. But
its light was already turned toward another season.

The voices of the junk dealers came on the wind through
the trees from the direction of the flea market. And the wind
smelled like old clothes and dust.

The flea market was one of the many places forgotten by
the city, where poverty disguised itself as business.

Weeds from regions where nobody lives grew in those
places: stinging nettles, thistles, yarrows. They were the other
country's weeds for Irene.

Irene got frightened when she saw the other country's
weeds here in the city. She had the suspicion that she had
brought the weeds over in her head. Irene touched the weeds to
make sure they were not her imagination.

Irene had another suspicion, too. That she kept her homesickness small and tightly woven in her head so she wouldn't
recognize it. That she undercut her melancholy as it manifested
itself. And that she built constructions of thoughts on her senses
to overwhelm them.

Thomas had worn a green silk shirt that Sunday. The silk had the color of the nettles. It caught the wind.

There had been a closeness between Thomas and Irene because of this shirt that had the color of nettles and because Irene was looking for nettles among the weeds.

Irene had felt that closeness. But no thought about it had gone through her head.

Stefan had talked a lot. Thomas talked little. Irene had hardly heard his voice when he said his name. She hadn't caught his name.

Stefan had repeated it loudly and clearly. Too loudly and too clearly for Thomas's indifference.

Stefan had talked about Palestinians. About rubber bullets. About Israelis and guard dogs.

Stefan had picked up a little stone from the ground. The piece of metal in the middle of the rubber bullet would be as big, he said. And deadly.

Cars were rushing through the sentences. Crooked reflections lay on the water of the canal. The seagulls didn't hear the noise anymore. They were walking around. They were filthy, voracious, and disheveled.

Irene saw Rosa Luxemburg. Her face lay on the water, black and gray, with pores made of newspaper.

Thomas had taken the small stone out of Stefan's hand. He was carrying it.

Thomas hadn't slept for two nights. He had left his friend. Or his friend had left him. Stefan didn't know for sure.

Coffins of relationships, Stefan told Irene later. These damned good-byes. Everybody knows it has to be. Nobody knows why.

Thomas had moved to one of the streets where you could see the Wall, Stefan said.

Irene knew those streets. Short men stood behind mountains of leaves and vegetables. The fruit was shining because the streets were so narrow. Oranges dazzled the eyes.

The streets were so narrow there, it was as if you walked up a mountain.

Thomas would pull himself together again, Stefan said. He had been through a lot. He had a marriage behind him.

At that time Thomas wasn't consistently gay, Stefan said. He had loved a woman for a couple of years.

And that Thomas had given up the bookstore. And that he had left this nest, Stefan said.

But the child, because Thomas had had a son with this woman. Stefan hadn't said anything about the child's situation.

It's been three years, Stefan said. Since then Thomas had been out of work for three years.

The closeness between Irene's eyes looking for nettles and Thomas's green silk shirt had begun on that Sunday when Irene had met Thomas.

Irene hadn't heard Thomas's voice then. And she hadn't noticed his face either because his thoughts had been so far away then.

Later, when Stefan had told her about Thomas, Irene knew that Thomas's hair was light. And that it had blown in the wind. Sometimes close to the bushes.

Thomas called unexpectedly a couple of days later. He was shy. Maybe he talked because he was shy about himself.

Irene was familiar with what he said. Stefan had told her this. But she liked to listen. Irene liked to listen to changes between facts: the small town, the wife, the child, the bookstore.

The same sentence—I loved a woman for a couple of years—sounded different.

At the end of the first conversation Thomas had already asked the question he had asked after every subsequent conversation. This question was out of place in the conversation now too, as it had been then. And Thomas asked now too, without any transition, as he had then:

Are you afraid of me.

Irene had not been scared of this question, not even in the first conversation. She had been prepared for the question without knowing it.

Her answer to this question was no every time. Thomas would hang up after that.

Once Thomas hadn't hung up. He had gone a step further.

I'm afraid of you, Thomas had said.

Irene hadn't been scared of this sentence either. She had asked in a calm, almost absentminded voice:

Why.

Thomas had answered in the same calm voice:

Because you see through me.

Thomas never invited Irene over.

One day Irene had gone a step further when Thomas had asked his question at the end of the conversation. After she had quickly said no, as usual, she said:

I want to come over.

But Thomas had expected this sentence:

When.

Now.

Thomas said:

OK.

Irene picked up a chestnut leaf on the street because her hand felt suddenly so empty.

The stairwell was narrow. There was an echo in it.

Irene rang. She looked for a spot on the threshold. The leaf was yellow. The threshold was dark.

Thomas opened the door. He took the leaf out of Irene's hand:

Where does the leaf come from.

Thomas wasn't expecting an answer. He rubbed the leaf lightly across his cheek. He walked into the room in front of her.

Irene stood in the doorframe. She saw the window through another window. She didn't know why she had come.

Irene sat down on the only chair so that she would have to stay and not go. The chair stood by the desk.

There were many pictures of one and the same person on the desk. They were pictures of the young, dead politician. Irene had also cut out one of them. It was left over, it wouldn't fit into the collage on the kitchen wall.

Thomas looked over Irene's shoulder.

My case, he said.

How come.

I am like him.

He wasn't gay. And you have no power, said Irene. The chestnut leaf lay on the bed.

Thomas walked toward the leaf.

My relationships are all the same, he said. I'm dependent in the beginning. Later it's the other way around. I always have the power. I don't want it. And I say no for both of us when I have it. The other one submits. He feels for both of us.

Thomas was sitting on the bed. Irene was looking through the window. As long as you know, she said.

Thomas rubbed the leaf across his hand.

I forbade myself to wield power socially. I have had my

chances. I haven't taken them. I have this disposition. I've always known that I'm dangerous, and I have always concentrated on what I don't want to become.

If you know that, it's not true, said Irene.

There was a pair of green socks between the books on the shelf. They still had a price tag on them.

I've lived against myself for so long, said Thomas, that nothing has become of me.

The light fell across the pictures on the desk.

You can tell by my face, said Thomas, you can tell by my face.

The face shows it as clearly as if I had done everything I didn't do.

Irene held one of the pictures very close to her face.

Thomas laughed. He put the leaf on the bed and stood up: I'm just going to check on how I'm doing.

Thomas opened the closet door and looked at his face in the mirror:

I'm a jinx. I have never left a man because of another man. I always had my reasons.

Thomas had pulled back his lips. He looked at his teeth.

Have you left many so far, asked Irene.

Thomas nodded. He looked at his larynx.

Then you have looked for reasons.

I never looked for them, I just found them. I only knew they existed after I had found them. The bad thing is that my unhappiness is too big for me. I always have to take it to other people.

A scaffold had been standing in the courtyard for two days. It had nine floors. It reached up to the roof. Boards covered the ninth floor. A corridor.

The courtyard looked even deeper with the scaffold in place. And narrower. It made that noise of wood and iron: high and low sounds alternating.

The noise remained dull. Monotonous. It captured its own shrill sounds.

The noise started at seven o'clock in the morning and lasted till early afternoon. This was a working day. Irene participated in it with her eyes.

The scaffold was actually about Irene and Franz. The scaffold had broken the silence in the courtyard. But the apartment still lacked a street under its window. The elder bush grew fast. New impulses tried to conjure up landscapes in the morning.

The elder bush was caught up in the relationship between Irene and Franz: fearful like her, unpredictable like him.

At seven o'clock the men climbed on the scaffold. One of them was young. He had shoulder-length hair and he wore a bandanna. His butt was wide and flat. His belly hung like a big pear under his shirt. The young worker looked like a fat child.

The worker sometimes whistled a song on the scaffold while working. The song was monotonous and subdued as if he were walking on the ground below. As if he weren't working, but only thinking and whistling.

Every day there were five workers on the scaffold.

Irene had picked one, the one with the bandanna and shoulder-length hair. He was the one she watched.

Irene didn't want to know more than she saw about him. She saw him participating in the noise on the scaffold. He raised his arms and lowered them. He took boards and pliers other workers handed him. He never looked anyone in the face. He was ugly and he didn't talk.

Irene only noticed the other workers when they were close

to the worker she had picked. But Irene didn't think about what they were doing. They were only there so the worker with the bandanna could work on the scaffold.

Franz would now be able to stand the courtyard, Irene thought. There is a scaffold here that changes every day. And behind the scaffold there is a wall that changes every day.

The bird that used to come to the courtyard often, but never stayed long, that made a mistake and often twittered in the wrong season, didn't come often now that the scaffold stood there. It had hardly landed before it flew away again. There was no time left for it to twitter. False tones came out when it opened its beak.

Franz would now be able to stand the lack of peace because there was no silence, Irene thought. Now he wouldn't say, You don't understand what I mean, you have good nerves. Franz could only say that in the silence.

The scaffold was silent in the afternoon. The worker Irene had picked had left. Every afternoon the scaffold looked as if he would never come back. As if he had made a mistake when he whistled, like the bird. But not a mistake in the seasons like the bird. A mistake between the floor and the depths.

The silence in the courtyard drove Irene out into the street.

Do you have any hand cream, asked the boy with the peaked cap.

No, said Irene.

He was leaning against a closed hot dog stand. He had an angry look.

Irene wasn't afraid of him anymore as soon as he began to talk.

Too bad. You women always have stuff like that in your purses.

I have some at home.

Where are you from.

It doesn't matter.

Irene walked away. She heard her steps stomping in her ears.

What does, the boy asked.

Thomas knew this boy with the peaked cap. He lived in every city. He was one of the many you lose track of while they are still alive.

They always leave their tracks behind, Thomas said. They don't take anything along from one corner to the other.

Thomas knew girls and boys who walked the streets.

They would let their skin shine for a couple of years. Their eyes would sparkle like wet stones. Their pupils were the hidden ends of drains, the semi-savage jewelry of rusty pipes.

Pupils, Thomas had said, pupils like earrings in the middle of the eyes.

The years withered fast around their thighs and hips. A touch of perfume mixed with a cloud of urine wherever they stood.

And later, what would happen later. What would become of them in the seasons that were coming toward them. When attics and basements would become too expensive. When they would no longer be allowed to make use of the city towers. When benches in subway stations would be transformed into chairs and iron doors would lock the entrances at night. When police patrols would sweep the halls of railway stations.

In spring and fall they would still have the corners between the trees and the tracks under the bridges. The benches in parks with plastic bags as pillows in summer. And dreams as long as the nights and the seasons. Dreams outside the head in which rats and rabbits, moles and birds would use the same entrances.

And in the winter when the red lights and the wailing sirens would come.

When the sleeping would wait, stiff in their limbs. And the policemen and doctors would no longer scream. They would roll out the tape measure and make drawings with chalk. And the passersby would gather around.

And on all these evenings music would come out of the bars as usual. The white ball would roll into the hole over green velvet tables, under lamps.

They are people that get to you through both good and bad, Thomas said. They are shady angels with their good side so reckless and their bad side so helpless that you can't deal with it. You need to look for another street if you see a shady angel.

Most people are lucky enough never to meet these creatures, Thomas said. I'm not. Or only a little. My bad luck is not so evident either. Every day I need to do something for my bad luck, against my will.

If you don't do anything for your bad luck, Irene said, you must be happy.

Bad luck has nothing to do with happiness, Thomas said. If I don't do anything for my bad luck the helplessness comes. It's like a stone, I can't move. Then I need to do something so it moves.

Irene wished she had given the shady angel with the peaked cap her hand cream at the hot dog stand. It was on the table next to the mirror.

ten

THE FASHION WAS LOUD IN THE BEGINNING OF
the seasons. And gaudy. Irene wished she had more bodies just
to wear all the clothes in the store windows. And money to buy
the clothes. And that you didn't have to buy the clothes, that
you might just borrow them, wear them for a few days until
you were tired of them. Ladies' stockings with seams lightly out
of place walked along the gutter toward the ends of street as if
women were legs only. Legs for men. They would catch eyes.
They also caught Irene's eyes.

Irene felt the skin on the back of her knees. And the
rhythms. Excitement drove Irene through the streets. The steps
were uneven, but light.

Everything Irene saw was a coincidence. It could have
been different. And it became different the very next moment.

Irene's hands became dry in the stores because she had no
money. And a bitter spot grew on the tip of her tongue.

Dust flew into her face between store windows.

But Irene was happy she had no money when she saw
three different women with the same barrette, an airplane, at
three different places in the city on the same day. And her hair
was too short for barrettes. And her head slowly became heavy.

And the skin between her nose and her mouth twitched like a big insect.

Then Irene knew: Fashion shortens your life.

The black lace underwear looked broken in the store window.

Irene imagined women walking in black lace into the bathroom or to the closet. And that you couldn't see the underwear at night.

And Irene knew women who despised black lace.

Pairs of white cotton underwear were hanging in their kitchens from the clothes racks. Irene knew that wouldn't work. That the excitement would still get to them, that they would know the cleft as well as the other women in black lace underwear who lay down in the breathing space between the hands of men.

The bell at the store door rang so often that it seemed as if Irene had entered the store three times. It rang twice when the door was already shut.

A short old lady stood behind the counter.

She opened her mouth as if to yawn. She didn't yawn. It was her way to line up the words in her mouth before she spoke.

Can I help you, she asked.

Irene's fingers reached between loose lace underwear. Black flowery designs lay on the back of Irene's hand.

The woman didn't take her eyes off Irene.

Irene's fingers inexorably went their own way. The woman watched as if she wanted to tell her off. As if she had used up all the love that had come to her when she had been young and smooth.

There was Franz's thumb between the underwear, among the fingers on Irene's hand.

Have you decided yet, the old lady's face asked.

Irene left Franz's thumb between the underwear.

The bell rang so loudly and so often as if the wind was blowing.

A thin woman pushed her way through the door. She carried a slim purse.

She quickly walked up to the shelves. She stopped in front of the perfumes.

She pushed her purse up her sleeve. She took a small bottle. She sprayed perfume behind both ears, on her neck, and on the collar of her coat. She looked to the left and to the right. She opened her purse and pulled out a handkerchief. She sprayed the handkerchief from both sides.

Irene stood behind her. The perfume rocked back and forth in the small bottle the woman put back on the shelf.

The fragrance was sweet. The old lady turned around. She had felt Irene's look.

In her face there was an arrogance pierced by wrinkles. And it was contempt pierced by wrinkles when she pushed her purse down her sleeve into her hand.

Irene opened the mailbox when she got home. The letters fell to the ground. There were ads in the mailbox.

Irene bent down. She reached for the letters. One ad said: The perfume that challenges your feelings. Every drop a temptation.

Irene smelled the letters. She recognized an envelope. It was from the other country.

Irene recognized the letters from the other country without looking at the stamps or the postmark. Irene recognized the rough, gray-white paper of the letters.

The letter came from Dana.

Dana's letters were always under way for many weeks. They had always already been opened before Irene opened them. The content of the letters was old. And carefully checked for what people were allowed to write. And for what they weren't.

The letters that challenge your feelings, Irene thought. Every drop a temptation.

Irene opened the letter and read the last sentence:

I miss you, I feel an almost physical longing for you.

Dana's voice came out of this sentence. And with that voice a breath that Irene knew didn't belong to Dana.

Irene often thought of the other country. But these thoughts didn't well up in her throat. They were not confused. They were comprehensible. Almost orderly. In her forehead, Irene could take them out. And push them back into the back of her head. Like files.

What had to move around in her head to be labeled homesickness.

Irene's thoughts remained dry. Tears never came.

Irene sometimes had the suspicion that she was both crumpled up and smoothly ironed.

She controlled her homesickness sorted by landscapes and states, officials and friends. It was the accounting of half her life: silent files on unknown shelves.

Irene could manage it. She was astonished and she knew she was astonished.

Irene had been living here for months. The months were in the calendar. There wasn't anything here that could prove it. Except for the seasons.

A season never ended without the next one starting with a slight variation.

Thermometers in drug stores on street corners rose and fell.

The chestnut tree in the side street was barren, then white, then green.

And from time to time there was a noiseless, jerky movement under her ribs as if sand were shifting.

There was an emptiness in her stomach that crawled into her mouth. A split in her calves like runs in stockings. That's what Irene couldn't see in the mirror.

But she saw the fear that one day the body would let itself fall down without warning its head in advance.

Maybe homesickness has nothing to do with the head, Irene thought. Maybe it exists independently and is caught up in the structure of your thoughts. Maybe it is a feeling, if you know how it ends. And how you get rid of it. Like sometimes you feel too light on the streets and sometimes too heavy.

If this is homesickness, Irene thought, I must be fake.

Stefan put thick files on the table.

A research project, he said.

His face was so pale that his temples looked like paper.

Irene stubbed out the cigarette. Stefan looked into the ashtray. A piece of blazing heat lay there, smoking on.

Irene had pulled her hand back under the table and onto her knee so fast, as if she had left.

You know, said Stefan, there is nothing, absolutely nothing that connects me with my place of birth.

Irene knew the place from a different context. It was a small town where a writer lived. Irene had read his books.

A model train in the basement of my parents' house is all that connects me to this place, Stefan said.

Irene knew Stefan's father had died. His mother was alive. She was living by herself in that house.

The fact that Stefan didn't mention the one who was still alive struck Irene as an omission at that moment.

The man at the next table draped the end of his gray scarf over his shoulder. He had heard what Stefan had said. He asked for a light and continued to listen.

I spent whole afternoons in the basement of that house, said Stefan.

Irene heard the noise of the model train and above it the steps of an old woman walking between objects across bare floors:

How old is your mother.

I still hear her talking when I come out of the basement, said Stefan. She doesn't talk to herself. She plays family. Mother, father, and child. She is not the mother either. Even the mother she plays is a different one. Not just to her but to me as well. She looks like a woman before a storm.

You know, I often go for walks along the streets before storms, said Stefan.

Women have the wind on their skin. They are distressed before storms. They look as if they know what the next years have in store for them. They were at risk.

It's the fear of aging, said Stefan. Their necks grow long and their hands a touch too white

The man with the gray scarf bent forward.

Their steps are unsure as if they lean their legs against the sky.

Stefan talked too loudly.

I'm careful with the key ring. I don't want to scare her when we go to my apartment.

Stefan looked around:

I pull out the bed and talk. I talk endlessly about things that don't concern me.

Stefan's mouth was wet:

I lie next to unknown skin when the first rain drops fall. Women are transparent when the bed gets warmer. One thing is not pleasant. I hear a rushing inside their heads when I kiss them.

Irene pushed up her sleeve. She looked at her watch. Instead of hands Irene saw an endless connection on the dial.

A jerky movement distributing itself equally over things that were present and people who were absent.

eleven

IRENE WAS ON HER WAY TO THE AIRPORT. IRENE
was on her way to Franz. She was happy to leave the city.

Five people were sitting in the subway train. All of them
had hands that were too big. All of them looked into the void.
The train jerked. Their heads nodded. Only their heads.

The two sitting across from Irene knew each other's smallest gestures. Which was why they always did everything wrong
for each other.

Pushy and firm, the young man had taken on the role of
the father vis-à-vis the old one. And the old man had taken on
the role of the son.

The father put his head on the son's shoulder. His eyes
were not sad. They had no shine. They were just dull.

The son spoke fast and softly. There was a plastic bag next
to him. He took a ziplock bag out of the plastic bag.

There were slices of bread and three eggs inside.

The son read the name of the station out loud.

The father had closed his eyes. He breathed as if he were
used to sleeping everywhere.

You shouldn't sleep now, said the son, do you hear me, you
are not allowed to sleep now.

He took an egg out of the ziplock bag. He began to shell the egg without looking at it. In his hand he collected the small, pointed pieces he broke from the shell.

When the egg was naked he put the shells in his pocket as if he were used to eating everywhere.

The egg was a nuisance to him. He held it in front of his father's face. The father was a nuisance to him.

I can't eat, said the father, do you hear me, I can't eat now.

He didn't open his eyes when he said that.

All you do is sleep, my God, do you ever sleep.

The son let the naked egg fall into the bag:

I'm leaving you here, do you hear me, I'm going to let you sit here.

The light was gray when Irene stepped out into the street. Only the dam was light. Behind the dam the sun was squashed between the sky and the grass. All the cars drove under the earth. A bird fluttered above the dam. It swerved away at the last moment. Because the light was dazzling. The clouds were crumpled and the tree moved its branches.

The airport stood behind the dam where the sun was squashed.

The travelers in the airport hall were confused. Their voices were muffled when they talked to each other.

The travelers reached for their suitcases as if something unpredictable were about to happen. They walked slowly. The stuff you need most is out of your reach when the crash comes.

Irene didn't sit down on the seat allocated to her by the boarding pass.

A man was sitting on the seat next to her. He had small red wounds at his cuticles. He had cut his fingernails in a rush, shortly before the trip. He was afraid the fingernails would grow faster on the road than at home.

He had also had a recent haircut.

The flight attendant pointed toward the emergency exits with her thumbs. She said passengers should follow the red lights to reach the emergency exit doors.

Irene wondered why it had to become dark before the crash. It was still morning.

Irene had stolen a sign from a construction site in the other country. A man was falling head down on it. The sign said: Danger—Falling into the Void.

Irene had hung the sign in her room in the other country. Above the bed. She had connected the warning to her life. And to the lives of everyone she knew.

The sign had hung for many years next to another sign that Irene had stolen from a road. There was a man with a shovel on it. On that sign Irene had written: Digging is always on the edge of the legal. It was a sentence from a book.

Irene had connected that sentence to her life too.

The flight attendant's mouth was smiling.

Irene sat by the window. She wanted to see the clouds and her fear. And her fear out on the clouds.

She couldn't tell Franz's face from the fear and the clouds.

The flight attendant carried a coffeepot through the aisle.

Excuse me, your heart has stopped, Irene heard her voice saying.

Her mouth didn't move.

Irene knew she was visiting Franz half against his will.

She perceived the length of the short street as depth. The leaves were wet. Cars were parked on sidewalks. Windows were lit behind gardens. They were so dark you couldn't see the color of the leaves. Only the edges were illuminated.

Big, yellow leaves covered the parked cars. The roofs, the trunks, the windshields.

The leaves were not wilted. They were as if freshly cut, with long, reddish stems.

And the coat of leaves covering the sidewalk was so soft. Irene didn't let on that she was freezing. She didn't force an embrace. She wasn't sure she was freezing either. It could have been the heat too. Or frost and heat at the same time.

Irene stopped in front of one of the parked cars. She said:

They are like graves.

Franz didn't say anything. His mouth moved. His chin was pointed. And his long, dark gray coat disappeared on the pavement.

One hour later the hotel room was too small and the walls much too white.

Strange, said Franz, that you think of graves when you see leaves.

Irene put her hands on the windowsill. The street was brightly lit. The bar door opened slowly. A drunk came out in the street.

A car parked.

The parked cars seem decorated, said Franz.

A woman got out of the car. She slammed the door.

One is my picture, the other one is yours, said Irene. There is nothing in between.

The woman ran the tip of her finger over the windshield wipers.

That's why I didn't contradict you, said Franz.

Irene saw his eyes reflected in the windshield.

You scared me, said Franz.

Irene looked briefly into the room. The match lay where she had put her purse.

The jacket slid from the woman's right shoulder. It remained hanging on her left shoulder.

I told you what I saw. I didn't mean to scare you, said Irene.

A man was sitting behind a newspaper. A woman wearing a wine-red jacket put a piece of meat on an empty plate in front of the man.

The man looked at the piece of meat and read on. That was happening on the screen.

Franz turned down the volume when the woman began to speak. Irene had the feeling that Franz didn't want to give her the right to speak. Irene looked at the woman's mouth. She didn't know what she was saying. But Irene knew she should have said to Franz what the woman was saying. As soon as the woman spoke without volume and the man ate the piece of meat, the wine-red jacket was so stiff and beautiful on the screen, and as pointless as a wine-red hat.

Franz was sitting on the chair, crumpled.

The wine-red jacket moved the chair and the floor into an angle meant only for faraway things. And Irene saw what Franz must have seen: that everything the woman in the wine-red jacket did was meant against Franz.

That didn't bother Irene. What did was the woman emphasizing her movements so clearly between what she was doing.

She knows how to blackmail. You either can do it, or you never try.

Irene was waiting for Franz in the street.

A man was begging. The woman standing in front of the store window looked at hats. She didn't give him anything. The man shouted.

He stood in front of her holding out his hand when Irene pressed two coins into it.

If you don't smile, said Irene, nobody will give you anything.

And if I say I'm thirsty, said the man. Only hunger works.

Franz pulled Irene by her sleeve.

You've given him something, you believed him, he said.

He is thirsty, said Irene, he didn't lie.

Franz bent down to her. His face was cold. And his eyes wet. He passed his hand through Irene's hair.

Franz was cautious. And the skyscraper behind him was made from glass. It was shining. And Franz was a little confused.

He is a different person in every city. Marburg doesn't reach here, Irene thought. Maybe he likes Frankfurt.

Then a café, a second and a third. The last one was poor and all black. Even the cups and the saucers. And mirrors all around. And every time between sentences Franz raised his glass to his mouth when it was already empty. And he talked a lot. And he often looked at his hands.

Then the river and the bench. A bench and no bed. Franz looked at the water and said: I like to touch you.

Then, in the dark, the gay pickup zone along the path between the leaves through which you could see the lights from afar.

Irene didn't know if Franz knew where he was. But she realized that Franz and she didn't belong there. Because the people waiting disappeared like shadows in the bushes after they had seen the strange pair she and Franz made. They would have waited for Franz if he had been alone.

Irene thought of the loose summer in the other country. Of the bush and the man who had said: Don't run away. I won't do anything to you. I only want to see you.

And Irene thought of the drummer.

There was more wood on the branches than leaves. And the people waiting hadn't disappeared. There was a rustling behind them even though there weren't any leaves. Or was it the wood making that noise, rubbing against eager skin.

Franz walked in front of Irene. Irene saw his back.

Irene thought: Now he's changing. Now he's becoming gay on the path between the leaves and the wood because he's walking through these images.

And it was jealousy that forced Irene to look to the ground with each step. Irene wanted Franz and wished he was gay, and forgot that she was a woman, not a man.

And the word that applied to women came to her mind. Irene didn't like the word.

And there was no wish there either to go with the word.

Kiss me, Irene would have liked to say to Franz. She didn't say anything.

Irene saw Franz to the railway station.

Trains on tracks. The stockings were mustard yellow. The girl's backpack was blue. Music broke away from her headphones. Heavily made-up eyelids. The eyes open and fixed as if they were never arrested by an image.

A sphere turned above the platform. It was illuminated from the inside.

Two women were talking to each other. They raised their hands between their faces as they talked. Their hands resembled each other. You could only distinguish them by the rings and the color of the nail polish. Then the hands pushed the suitcases closer. The lips were open and said nothing.

A pair of black dress shoes was shining. It reflected nothing but a pair of white socks.

A dove tripped next to the train. It carried its head so stiffly Irene didn't know if it was tortured by arrogance or illness.

The tracks were swollen with light where there were no trains. Wooden beams in between. Ground stones between the beams. Cigarette butts.

The dove was hanging in the air above the stationary train. Irene saw a cogwheel behind its beak.

If Irene had wanted to say what she felt, no sentence would have been accurate. Not even syllables that came together randomly.

The voice of a woman announced trains out of the turning sphere.

Beautiful lips high up announcing trains for dwarfs, Irene thought.

The girl with the mustard-yellow stockings got on the train. Her legs were heavier than her backpack.

I had a good time with you, Franz said.

Irene hadn't added anything. The good time had hurt Irene because it had been a good time and nothing more.

Irene went back to the hotel.

She turned on all the lights in the room. She turned on the TV and went into the bathroom. She washed her underwear and her pantyhose. She hung the underwear on the back of the chair and the pantyhose on a hanger on the closet door.

A small town passed across the screen.

The inhabitants of the small town were commuters. The way to the railway station led through the vineyard.

In the twilight hours of the evening young women coming from the city walked home from the station through the vineyard.

Eight women had been raped in the vineyard.

The wrongdoers: two men.

The announcer named their first names. He showed a

knife. It was the one they had used to force the women to do what they wanted.

The speaker announced a number. That was the price on their heads.

The pictures of the ghosts were on the screen.

Because of the prices on their heads, it would have been impossible for Irene to do justice to the victims even if she had known the wrongdoers.

The trust in the vineyard, excessive on the part of both wrongdoers and victims, hurt Irene more than the deed.

The air in the room was old. Older than the furniture.

Irene opened the window.

Irene had forgotten the name of the hotel now that she leaned out. And also the name of the river running through the city. And the name of the bridge spanning the river.

COLD COUNTRY COLD HEARTS JUST CALL ME JENS. And a phone number.

It was a graffito on the wall of a house, up above the trees. The writing was running down the wall. Letters with fingers. Passersby walked across the square and felt the effect of the writing without raising their heads. For a few steps they would put their hands in their pockets. They would freeze a little without knowing why.

Irene imagined the man named Jens as younger than herself, as old as Franz. And she imagined herself as a child in the other country. The name Jens was fashionable here in the cities when names like Franz were popular in the other country.

Irene's eyes had left the square. Male mannequins in store windows accompanied her, stylish and blond, smiling artificially.

A weight was hanging in Irene's knees. And in her forehead a wish that almost included the whole city.

COLD and COUNTRY and HEARTS. Irene had forgotten the phone number. And JENS.

The phone rang briefly. Then a child's voice answered.
JENS, said Irene.
Mommy, the child called, it's the woman from yesterday.
There was a click. And then an empty humming.
Travelers, Irene thought, travelers with their nervous eyes on the sleeping cities. On wishes that are no longer valid. They have their sights set on the inhabitants. Traveling on one leg, lost before they change to the other.
Travelers are always late.

We have proved that, if we existed, we wouldn't be, said Franz.
Irene saw the numbers on the dial. They were ticking. No, it was the clock.
If we existed together, said Irene, paired.
The sentence is a quote, said Franz.
Irene saw the quiet scaffold:
Whose quote is it.
The worker Irene had picked had painted a windowframe green early in the afternoon.
I don't know, said Franz. I also forgot the title of the book. I don't even remember what it was about. Not about love.
The worker Irene had picked hadn't whistled for the last few days when he stood on the highest floor. He carried a small, red radio in the pocket of his pants. It sang for him. He reached into his pocket and searched for another station when it began to speak.
The worker listened to hits, rock music, and big band music.
I know how you can forget whole books, said Irene. Only individual, audacious sentences are left over. They belong to

you as if your own experience had whispered them to you in a railway station. As if they came to your mind against your will.

Railway stations, said Franz. I think this book was about cities.

You transform these sentences, you make them into what you are, said Irene. You think you can live off these sentences because they are audacious.

There were spots of paint next to the green painted window. The worker Irene had picked had tried out nuances between gray and dark green.

But after a couple of years you get tired of these sentences. They sound very normal when you say them out loud. And no unknown voice, said Irene. Only your own. A few words that otherwise you wouldn't say out loud. Like a picture of yourself with a strange expression. Its audacity is lost.

Audacious, I like that word, said Franz.

Why grass green, Irene thought. She looked at the paint spots.

Then came Franz's last sentence because he said: I wish you something.

This sentence didn't wish for Irene what she wished for herself.

Irene tried to repeat the sentence Franz had said first. She had forgotten it:

If we existed. And what came before, and what afterward. It was a sentence that didn't belong to Irene. That she wouldn't have noticed in a book.

The next morning the mailman brought an express mail letter:

If you would see the city from the inside, it would be different. Irene is a name of a faraway city, if you get close to it it becomes different. It's one city if you go by and don't enter it, and another if you get moved by it and don't leave it. It's one city if you come to it for the first time and another if you leave it, never to return. A different name for each. Maybe I talked about Irene using different names. Maybe I only ever talked about Irene.

I didn't write one word of this. I quoted, Franz wrote. The title of the book is: *The Invisible Cities*. I marked the passage about the city Irene years ago. I didn't connect it with any person at that time. That your name is Irene scares me now, it really does.

twelve

IRENE WAS SITTING IN THE WAITING ROOM OF the Admission Facility. Her waiting number was 501 even though there wasn't anybody else waiting besides her. Irene heard the retching of the coffeemaker behind the door. And the official's voice. A slow voice taking breaks between words.

A secretary opened the door a crack. She waved her in. She wore a green silk blouse. She kept her hand on the doorknob.

Irene slipped shoulder first through the crack of the door and into the office. The secretary pointed to a chair next to the window.

The official was sitting at his desk. He drank coffee. There were no papers on the desk. A coffee cup and a piggy bank stood on the desk.

The official puckered his mouth before he swallowed the coffee. He looked out the window.

A truck was rushing outside between the trees.

A Pole, said the official.

He had jumped up with the coffee cup in his hand. He knocked with his fingertips on the pane:

He is still here as you see.

You're right, said the secretary.

Maybe you mistake him for somebody else, said Irene.

The secretary plucked a leaf from a tired plant.

The official was drinking while standing:

No residency, no working permit. Nothing. He looked at the secretary's hand that squashed the leaf. He took a step over Irene's shoes. Irene pushed the shoes under the chair. He put the coffee cup on the desk only after he had sat down.

If you want to mistake a person for another you need two. At least two. You don't know how I remember faces. You can be certain that I'll retire and still know all of them. Mistaken for whom.

For another Pole, the secretary laughed.

You're right, we have enough of those.

For a German, said Irene, maybe for a German driver.

Irene saw the crack in the coffee cup and the official's thumb.

The secretary opened a drawer:

I beg your pardon, but you've seen this face. He is politically persecuted. You know, if someone wants to overthrow the government. What's the world coming to. You see what I mean.

The lady is also from the East, said the official.

The secretary leafed through Irene's papers:

Don't make me laugh.

She didn't laugh.

Irene woke up sweaty as if she had run out of this dream.

Other pictures came together:

The official in the subway. He got on behind Irene. He had taken off his hat before he got on. What was he doing here with his expensive hat in this neighborhood. Where even trees are broken into.

The official sat down next to Irene. He asked Irene a question.

Irene answered in the language of the other country. This was another dream on the same night.

The official put his expensive hat on his knees. He grabbed Irene's elbow.

That's what I thought. You only speak German when you come to my office.

Irene had forgotten the German.

Irene could have spoken only one single sentence in German: Why do you always compare, it's not your native language. Thomas had spoken that sentence.

It would have been a long sentence. It would have proved that Irene spoke German. But it would have done more harm than good. Irene knew that even in her dream.

Dreams have their reasons, Thomas had said when he had told her his licorice dream.

First there was this uneven street. Then a village with scattered one-story houses. You know, houses that should have been condemned. Then I saw my wife and my son at a birthday party for children. There were more adults than children there. All adults were women. And all children were little girls. Just now it occurs to me that my son was a little girl too. All the women and all the little girls were eating licorice snails. Licorice was all they had at this party. They all had their mouths full. Their cheeks and their hands too. Everywhere you looked there were licorice snails: on the table, on the chairs, under the table, under the chairs. The women rolled them up, knotted them, and ate them. The little girls played train with the rolled-up licorice snails.

I wouldn't wish such a dream on anyone, said Thomas, not even on an enemy.

Irene passed the back of her hand over Thomas's cheek:
Do you have enemies.

Thomas shrugged his shoulders.

You don't have a job, you seldom go to the authorities. What you do is private.

Thomas thought about it. He said: Yes.

He spoke slowly as if he didn't know the next word yet:

I have friends. And all my friends are my former or my future enemies.

Have you counted me in there too, Irene asked.

I don't know, I haven't counted at all.

Do you know the game, Thomas asked:

A flock of sheep on a meadow. A shepherd and a sheepdog guard the sheep. Literally speaking, the shepherd is guarding the sheepdog, not the sheep. A wolf, a fox, and a tiger waylay the sheep in the forest behind the meadow.

Thomas illustrated everything he said with his hands.

A lady poodle stands to the side, next to the tree on the meadow. A bunch of flowers lies next to the lady poodle. The lady poodle is white, said Thomas. The sheepdog is torn between his duty to guard the flock and his love for the lady poodle. He has to drive away the wild animals when they come close to the flock before it is too late. And he has to give the lady poodle the bunch of flowers to prove his love to her. And all that without being seen by the shepherd.

Of course I like to play the game against myself, said Thomas. He pointed at himself:

The first game is the best one. I earn many points. Then I play again and lose. In the end it's not a game. It's a defeat.

Of course I'm always the sheepdog. I can always cast different people as the wild animals for each game. The lady poodle too. And the shepherd. But I mostly cast pimps. My relationships change through the game every day.

As a sheepdog, said Thomas, I naturally never get devoured. Worse things happen to me: I get worn down. And I have a guilty conscience no matter what I do.

The game was no bigger than a calculator.

Let me be the sheepdog, said Irene.

She pressed the red button.

The wolf devoured a sheep. The shepherd turned around in circles. The sheepdog chased away a fox.

Don't forget the lady poodle, said Thomas.

Irene laughed:

I can't understand the sheepdog, I think the lady poodle is repulsive.

The tiger devoured a sheep.

Thomas took the game out of Irene's hand:

You have to feel like the sheepdog. You have to love the lady poodle, otherwise you're playing a different game.

Irene took the only yellow apple from the fruit tray. Its skin was wrinkled.

Take the peach, said Thomas.

He held the peach up to the window, against the light. Irene shook her head.

The banana is yellow too, said Thomas.

Yellow, but not wrinkled

Then take a fresh apple.

The pictures of the young dead politician were not on the desk anymore.

Did you throw the pictures away.

Thomas held a green apple in his hand. He nodded.

The one with the white roots of the nails too.

Removed. That was really my case. I know men in those circles. Men in a manner of speaking. I know two. Two diplomats. Know in a manner of speaking. I knew. Holger and Joachim. At that time I still had my bookstore. I visited them both. Holger somewhere in the East. Joachim in Mozambique. Both were obsessed. Holger with his icons. Joachim with his ivory. They had only one thing on their minds: how to make off with more icons and more ivory.

Irene's look passed over the spines of the books on the shelf.

We couldn't find an end in the nights, said Thomas. The servants would come when it got bright in Maputo. The beggars a little later. They were half children. The table was full of glasses. They were sticky from our fingers. I felt paralyzed when I heard the servants screaming and throwing objects. They drove out the beggars. They threw shoes, and rags, and brooms at them until you couldn't see them anymore.

Joachim and I went down to the harbor around noon. We had met right before in a narrow street. Joachim came from the embassy, it was his lunch break. I saw him from afar. Who else would wear a suit there. Beggars lay on the side of the street. Some of them were howling, others were just lying there. Joachim didn't know either if they were just sleeping. He felt uncomfortable when I asked him. The heat flickered above the city. Joachim's piano had arrived in the harbor after a long journey. The path was rocking back and forth where the ship was moored. We stood there on spindly legs after a sleepless night. The piano was only half wrapped up now. It was shining next to the water. The harbor was empty. Joachim walked back and forth, sweaty and vigilant. He smiled from time to time. I saw the piano keys in his mouth. Who knows, said Thomas, what he saw in my face. I only served the forbidden passions of a diplomat. A piano owner and an ivory hunter. I remember his letters in which he addressed me formally so our relationship wouldn't be obvious. I hated myself. Joachim went back to the embassy. I was supposed to guard his piano until the pickup truck came. I didn't see any pickup truck anymore. After an hour I left on the first ship with no luggage.

I like wrinkled apples, said Irene.

Thomas looked out onto the street.

Irene touched his hand with the apple:

The apple tastes flat. It produces an aftertaste while you have the bite still in your mouth.

That's how it looks, too. Flat. You're chewing so slowly because you don't like it.

It doesn't taste like an apple. I don't know what it tastes like. The apple feels on my tongue like the sun on the back of my head in late fall. You only feel it when you walk in the other direction.

I haven't seen a flock of birds in ages. In the evening between houses. Before I used to show them to my son. My God, what do they feel when they change direction so often in the evening.

Thomas pointed to the sky:

They are flying to the Wall.

Two birds are not a flock, said Irene, maybe a pair.

In those days their were flocks.

Thomas put his hand on Irene's neck:

Don't say pair. Look, they are shining like flying leaves.

Irene swallowed a bite. She felt Thomas's fingers hot on her skin as she swallowed. Irene ate the core.

Leaves of foliage or of paper, she asked.

She held the stem of the apple in her hand.

When you eat an apple it's gone all right.

Irene laughed and pulled her neck out of Thomas's hand.

Thomas raised his eyebrows.

Now you're going to get wrinkled, first your stomach, then your throat, then your face.

Irene got scared. She put her hand on her cheek:

The apple has no effect yet.

Her voice was unsure:

In the other country there are two different words for leaves. One for foliage and one for paper. You have to decide what you mean there.

Irene saw wrinkled skin on her hands. Thomas looked at his hands:

Yes, they speak another language there. Why do you always compare. After all it's not your native language.

You have said so very often.

Irene wanted to add something. Instead she threw the stem of the apple out of the window. She watched it fly down.

Then Irene lay naked in the bed next to Thomas. Hot waves under the skin, a red washed-up condom. Everything else was washed away out of her head.

It had gotten dark outside. The window was shimmering.

Irene slowly put on her clothes. She wanted to remember how she had gotten naked. She smelled of sweat and traces of perfume. And she wished she didn't exist.

Thomas put the pillow against the wall.

I thought you were gay. I know it for a fact.

Sometimes I make exceptions, Irene, I still had to make love to you quickly before you get too many wrinkles.

Irene looked for her second shoe. It was under the desk. Irene slipped it on and knew: She had dropped the shoe. They had been sitting on the desk. Thomas had said:

You have nice toes.

Maybe men who love men say those kinds of sentences, Irene had thought. Men who love women don't say those kinds of sentences.

Thomas pulled the blanket over his shoulders.

Everything ends up in bed, said Irene.

She saw Thomas's hair against the white wall.

Let's not talk about it. Or let's talk about it if you want to. So talk.

It really doesn't matter if we talk or don't. If we talk about wrinkled apples, or flocks of birds, or your diplomats, or your male prostitutes. It doesn't concern us, Thomas. We basically always think about things that concern us. We actually use all our thoughts not to say them. We think about things that concern us even when we talk about the weather. One of us always thinks about them. The other one feels it. I'm tired of it, Thomas, and I can't change it.

That's mean, said Thomas.

Irene combed her hair in the dark:

Mean would be good. But it's terrible, and it's not a lie.

The sky was brighter than the sidewalk. It seemed to be illuminated.

We aren't shady angels, Thomas, we are just shady.

The pillow had slipped away from the wall. Thomas rested his chin on his knee:

What are you going to do now, Irene.

Irene heard steps on the sidewalk. She walked to the window. She only saw the cigarette. It was so white that it guarded the sidewalk with its color. Parked cars. No steps, but this noise.

Outside the night walked back and forth in front of the

window. Irene had the feeling that this night and this city were playing cop and robber. Wrongdoer and victim like her, like them.

Irene drew the curtain:

We yelled, Thomas.

Thomas took Irene's hand and pulled her toward him onto the bed:

Yes, we yelled at each other.

The wrinkled apple is working. I feel burnt out.

Irene put on her jacket.

Have you noticed how often we call each other by our first names when we don't like each other. We fear for each other.

Irene picked up her purse:

It doesn't make us better than we are. I want to go now.

You are lucky. You can go home now. I am at home.

Thomas turned on the light. He put the room and himself brightly in her way. She pushed him aside:

I need to rush so I won't be angry with you.

Eyes like stoplights. Then a cold safety overcame Irene. As if she were walking over shining paper, an object moving from one postcard to another. And everything she wanted to think about disappeared. Whole trains of thought were in her head, like the trams in the streets.

A man was walking between the driving cars in the straggly light. He walked on the white stripe that divided the road into different directions. His face was dark. His shoes were shining. His jacket fluttered in the wind and the headlights of the cars were shining on the teeth of his zipper like blurry circles.

The rectangle was bright in the courtyard. The woman without the blouse was talking and moving her hands in front of her face. The shadow of a bucket stood on the scaffold. Then the town hall clock struck behind the roof.

The day had begun four hours before.

The water in the shower came in thrusts. The skin hurt as if someone were throwing sand.

Now, as she stood naked in the light and bent down, Irene was surprised that her shoulders didn't fall on her toes.

The floorboards creaked in the hallway.

The man sitting under the empty sky in the collage on the kitchen wall looked straight into Irene's face when she turned off the light.

thirteen

THE WOMAN READ THE DESCRIPTION ON THE
back of the package. She put the soap in the shopping cart. It
was full of bottles, boxes, and cans. One package seemed to
take away the color of the other.

Irene looked away when the knot in her throat went up to
her mouth and she felt her temples beating in her ears.

Wool lay next to scissors and corkscrews. Braids of black
hair were hanging next to soup ladles.

Irene imagined the butcher behind the counter wearing a
black braid. He held his head to one side. The braid was heavy.
It must have been made of meat.

Irene walked by the bread. Advertising texts marched
through her forehead. Jingles: The young bride couldn't say "I
do" because Mrs. Baird's bread tastes true. Instead of young
bride Irene said white bride. She was looking for another
rhyme. The white bride couldn't say "I do" because she was too
excited to. Then Irene looked for all the white things in the
store: toilet paper, diapers, pads, cotton balls, tampons. Sliced
bread: A bride as white as sliced bread, Irene said to herself.

A radish fell through the bars of a shopping cart pushed by

a man. The man bent down. He let the radish fall into his coat pocket.

The cash register rattled at the end of the aisle.

The cashier looked through Irene out to the street. She must have hurt her finger recently. She looked at the wound on her finger as she rang up the numbers on the cash register.

Irene pushed the empty shopping cart past the cash register. Irene was happy: if you don't buy anything you must have stolen something.

The joy in her head was so big that it drove her brain out of balance. It was hot and stood diagonally in her head.

The shopping carts shone next to the exit. They stood close one behind the other. Each was pushed into the other's belly. The wheels were crooked.

Vegetables in front of the store door. The light shimmered over the oranges and the cauliflower. Irene had the feeling that lettuce, lemons, and mushrooms would run together in this light and that they would turn into flowers.

The man with the radish in his pocket went in the opposite direction.

Summer was all over the place like a long gap between thoughts that grew shorter and shorter.

People were lying on colorful sheets in the middle of the park. They were naked and their eyes were closed. If they moved an arm or a leg, or a wrinkle on their faces, they did so without meaning to.

A man passed by the colorful sheets. He looked at the people lying on them. He looked at the women longer than at the men. And even longer at the women lying by themselves on the sheets.

He was wearing a watch with a black dial.

The hands and the numbers shine at night, Irene thought.

The watch's edge was plated with gold. It burned in the sun so that a ray touched Irene's forehead like a shot.

The trees were turning upside down. For a while they stood on their crowns between the people lying around. Irene walked on her head.

A fly's shadow buzzed on Irene's arm. There weren't any flies there.

The gas station was behind the park. Above its roof it said: Day and Night. The walls were made of glass. Advertising yellow as dandelions, and no car, nobody there at noon.

A woman walked up to the gas station. She crossed the street, alone, where it was forbidden. Her belt buckle was shining.

On this day the sky was smaller than an eye.

Irene sat down on the grass.

She wrote a postcard:

Franz, I'm lying in the sun in the park. A widow is taking a turtle for a walk on a leash like a white thread. The widow's face is tired when she walks in the shade. And it's old when she is walking in the sun. And there's much peace in her face. I've seen the widow with the turtle before. In the same park, under the same trees. Maybe it was in the other country, or in another city. Maybe in a movie. It might be that I only imagined the two and that I'm doing it again now. But I'm surprised that they made it through the winter. This late summer. I waited so long for the sun to shine that it made me stupid and I forgot how to walk on dry surfaces. I'm tired and inwardly so awake that I cannot keep my eyes closed. I took off my stockings and my shoes. I watch my toes from afar. I don't want them to be mine.

Then Irene stood on the tips of her toes, on her own skull.
Irene put on her stockings and her shoes.

She walked the shorter way through the park. It was a gravel path covered with bushes.

Irene carried a bag. It rustled as if her legs and the path were thin and made of plastic. And the shoes not strong.

Irene could tell by the rustling of her bag that she was walking faster.

A man was sitting on the next bench. He put his hand like a funnel in front of his mouth and shouted: Georg. He shouted in all directions. His voice sounding between the same name.

The man looked straight into Irene's face. He was all eyes. He asked: Have you seen the electrician.

He said the word *electrician* in such a way as if one man were responsible for all the lights in the city.

Irene shook her head. She wanted to walk away from the bench faster than she thought. But the man was already walking over the gravel path across the grass.

Irene felt a small stone in her shoe. She reached into her bag. She felt a hand on her hand.

She avoided the chestnut tree in the side street. She imagined the street corner you couldn't see yet after you had avoided the chestnut tree.

When she had gotten to the street corner Irene imagined the next street corner.

The first person coming toward me around the next street corner will be a man, Irene thought. The first person was a woman.

Irene intentionally touched the woman's hand as she walked past her. The woman didn't notice.

Then Irene decided to ask the first person that she would meet after a hundred steps: Have you seen the electrician.

After a hundred steps Irene couldn't ask the man passing by the question.

Five times Irene couldn't ask that question of the first person who walked past her.

Then Irene had reached the railing of a bridge. She looked down at the city tram's rusty rails. A bird picked at a shoe that lay split open.

A man, walking slowly, came toward Irene from the other end of the bridge.

Irene waited for him. He looked down. Maybe he was listening to the sound of his steps.

When the man passed by her Irene looked into his ear:

Have you seen the electrician.

The man stopped right between two steps:

Not that I know of.

He closed his mouth and turned around.

Then Irene saw his back with one eye and the rails with the other.

And when the man's back had reached the first houses, Irene wasn't sure if it wasn't her walking slowly down the street.

Then the street was empty and the oblique light x-rayed the houses.

The bird had flown away.

The shadows of the trees lay on the asphalt like deep places. Behind them was the underpass.

And after the underpass, asked Irene. She wanted to answer with the man's sentence and give it more precision:

As I said, not that I know of.

Irene turned on the light in the hallway. She took off her shoes. She found a stone in her shoe. She took it into the room. She walked fast.

Irene expected the light to go out in the apartment because she didn't know who Georg was.

The pane reflected the lamp. Because it was dark outside the lamp was hanging in the middle of the courtyard again like a white ball on a cord.

Irene held the stone in her hand. She didn't know where to put it. She let it fall on the earth in the flowerpot.

There was an eyelash on the windowsill. Irene tried to blow it away. It was stuck to the wood.

Irene wet her fingertip and took it. She knew it wasn't hers. She threw it on the earth in the flowerpot.

A group was playing on TV. The music and the shining of the light touched each other. Irene was excluded.

She put her hands on the table and felt them on her forehead. And there was something else she felt: that she had lost everything in a moment that must have been decisive.

Irene didn't know when this moment might have been and how she could have recognized it. Irene didn't know what she had lost either.

Irene walked through the apartment and turned off the lights. First in the hallway. Then in the kitchen. Then in the bathroom. Then in the living room.

Irene was lying in bed; she had the impression that she could see the pupils of her own eyes shining.

Irene thought of the illuminated rectangle:

A small room, a night-light, a big bed in the corner. A refrigerator at the foot of the bed. The night-light was on.

A man lay naked in bed. The woman without the blouse stood at the foot of the bed. She pulled both her stockings and her panties down her legs in one movement.

She reached up at her neck. She opened the clasp of a

heavy, brown necklace. It had three rows of knots. She put the necklace on the refrigerator, she handled it carefully. She seemed to be completely preoccupied with the necklace as if she had taken off her clothes only to be able to take off her necklace.

She only looked very briefly at the bed, she smiled as if to herself. She slipped off her bracelet. It had three rows of brown knots. She put the bracelet next to the necklace on the refrigerator.

She bowed her head twice and from each earlobe she took an earring, another brown knot, and she put both earrings on the refrigerator.

The woman giggled, she opened the door of the refrigerator. A light as bright as the night-light went on, shining on her belly.

The woman took an empty tray out of the refrigerator. She put the necklace, the bracelet, and the earrings on the tray. She put the tray back into the refrigerator. She closed the door the same instant the man turned off the light.

The woman was moaning and the man was panting in the dark.

Then the light in the refrigerator went on, followed immediately by the nightlight.

The woman took the tray out of the refrigerator.

Slowly, fully preoccupied with herself, she put on the necklace, the bracelet, and the earrings as if she had slept with the man only to put her jewelry back on. The jewelry moved. The brown knots were living snails.

fourteen

WHAT HAVE YOU BEEN DOING FOR SO LONG,
asked Stefan because he had waited for Irene.

Irene said:

I didn't hurry.

Irene had lied.

Irene had put on makeup. She didn't want to tell Stefan that she had stood in front of the mirror to take care of the pores at the arches of her nose and the crumpled wrinkles in the corners of both eyes.

And that there had been something of a numbness as she hurried along with her fingers on the eye shadow, a numbness that had slowed everything down in its own way.

And there was mascara in the middle of her eyeball when the feeling came hot and cold to Irene's mind that there was always another woman behind this face.

The mascara burned in her eyeball.

Oh dear, said Stefan, they really tarted up the place.

When Stefan came from his office he said: I really let off steam. I really gave him hell, said Stefan when he had a fight with a man. When he had had a fight with a woman, he said: We went at it no holds barred.

Stefan suddenly turned around on the street. He looked back at a woman: sharp. He looked back at a man: cool.

Stefan would sometimes say: That can't be right, right. Or: I can't control myself anymore. Or: That's terrible, isn't it.

In between the sentences of others Stefan would say: Everything's OK. Great. Cool. Super. Sharp. Marvelous. And in between his own sentences he would say: Maybe.

In the morning I often wake up because the phone rings, said Irene. You can't get away from it. It's an order. It beats against my head until I wake up. I push myself to the phone. There is a discrepancy between the urgency in the ringing and the calm voice speaking afterward. I listen with my eyes closed, said Irene.

Nonsense, said Stefan, that's nonsense of course. And he said: You are too friendly. You are accessible to everyone. You don't choose the people you want. You'd be surprised what's out there.

Had Irene picked Stefan. Franz. She didn't know.

Look at you, said Stefan, you still have that smile from the East.

He kissed Irene on the cheek. Irene smiled:

Did you feel it.

What.

The smile from the East.

No, just that you're sad.

Stefan spoke of an answering machine.

If there is someone on the phone that you'd rather drop dead than talk to, just don't pick up.

Drop dead, he had said. Irene looked into his face:

I'll fight back. Not this way. It has nothing to do with dropping dead.

Stefan's eyes couldn't take these sentences. He laughed

with embarrassment. His face shrunk more and more, the longer Irene looked at him. His cheekbones were grinding.

This beating in my stomach, said Stefan. I'm always nervous when I'm on the way. Everything I see gets to my skin.

People traveling in groups are always nervous. Bureaucrats and secretaries, as if transformed. Do you know this euphoria, they always eat and laugh because they are so nervous. They have gas and hiccups and they throw out their nets. Their nervousness always wants to get to others, outside of the group.

They sneak to the rooms next door in the hotels when nothing has come along by bedtime. They creep through the halls at night. Do you know this creeping, the light shining by itself, the curtains half-drawn, railway stations shining close by. And all around station clocks bright like moons, no matter what direction the halls lead to. They shimmer through the curtain. You don't hear your own steps on the carpet, just the cracking of the elevator far down and the night clerk phoning softly from the reception desk. And everything you do is like a break-in.

It's not forbidden, said Irene, it's just your guilty conscience.

Stefan shook his head.

That's all on the bill, said Irene, that's anticipated, that's included in the figures even if you don't do it. The staff expects it. This and much more. I only know about washing stockings and panties in hotels, said Irene. Water running over your hands. The dark outside as if I had never seen the city. The foam gets so dark that I see the street again. I don't want to look anymore. I only look into the mirror and leave my face out of it. Then it stands there next to the toothbrush. The drain is sucking up the water. Later the dripping from the stockings on the hanger. It hangs at the closet door. The water stops for a while at the edge between the carpet and the closet. Then the drying of the panties at night when I plan to sleep against everything going through my head. Then the noises I hear as I'm half-asleep. Sometimes the closet or the chair cracking. The air smells of dusty blankets. I often turn on the light and wonder why pantyhose on hangers make the nights longer.

I immediately think of you, said Stefan, when I enter the city. I don't plan on it. But it comes up no matter how long I've been away. I'd like to put down the suitcase and call you. Then I'm in the big halls and nothing comes to my mind. I should be quiet. Stand here and be quiet.

It would be different with you, said Stefan. I can't imagine how it would be with you. I know you.

Curiosity, said Irene. It's curiosity with me, too. And something else that doesn't urge me on. It warns me.

Irene had gotten used to Stefan's pale face. Or maybe it wasn't pale after all. Only the shadows were dark. The grinding under his cheeks, no shadows there.

Irene had the feeling Stefan's grinding cheekbones would whisper something in his ear when he was quiet.

It's strange, said Irene, when you talk about women I'm many women at once. I don't know them. I am like them for as long as you talk. It's love used up, representing me. I don't get lonely, this warns me against you.

Stefan looked through his glass. The beer foam covered his eyebrows.

Stefan's mouth looked crooked.

I can feel you. You lean against the table and I feel you as if I were the table, he said.

Irene leaned her head against Stefan's shoulder. Her neck felt stiff. She let her head fall on his shoulder so unexpectedly as if it were bending with speed.

Irene said with her mouth on his coat:

Now I lean against you and I feel you as if you were the table.

Stefan raised her chin:

Who would believe you. Look at your neck.

I do it more and more. She broke up the sentence, she looked at the bar. Then she said as if it were a different sentence:

I feel more and more like afterward. I sit here together with people as if they had gone away a long time ago. You too.

Stefan kissed Irene's neck:

And you.

Stefan's glass was empty. The traces of foam were stuck to the edge. Stefan raised his glass and held it at an angle. The slice of lemon moved.

He kissed Irene's fingertips and looked up at the ceiling. His eyeballs were moving as if he were watching a circling object.

Imagine everyone had gone, said Irene. A man would sit alone in an empty bar and fake a kiss.

Stefan briefly looked at her. The redness in his eyes entered Irene's eyes.

Where, Stefan asked.

Irene pointed at his chair.

You called once at night, said Irene, I think it was in March. You were in a small hotel. Then you told me without transition that I was the only woman you hadn't cheated on yet.

I remember, said Stefan, I wanted to come to you. It might have lasted an hour or a moment. I don't know that anymore. I didn't know it then either.

Irene fell out of the bed that night.

Not because of the dreams.

Because of the other country where Irene's bed had stood against the long wall in the room. Here Irene's bed stood against the short wall.

What was the length of the bed in the other country was its width here.

Irene fell on the floor because in her sleep she was lying lengthwise across the width of the bed.

Irene got scared. She turned on the light.

She stood barefoot in front of the mirror. Her face hadn't gotten to the mirror yet. It was yellow.

Why did Irene laugh, why did she laugh in the morning when she talked about it.

fifteen

THE OFFICE LOOKED LIKE A HALL. THERE WAS A second door behind the desk.

The woman behind the desk looked like a receptionist. Irene didn't know whether it was the door or the woman's facial expression.

She read the notarized translations of the documents Irene had put on the edge of the desk.

Indoor ivy was hanging around the door frame. Small nails were holding it.

The originals, she said.

The receptionist put a paper clip between her lips:

German citizenship takes a while.

She tried to arrange the documents in a different order. The birth certificate was moving farther and farther to the back.

How long does it take, Irene asked.

The paper clip between the woman's lips moved:

No point in asking. You can't do anything to speed it up.

A phone was ringing behind the door with the ivy around it. It rang six times. It broke off. Irene didn't know whether the boss had picked up or the caller had given up.

You'll be notified, said the receptionist.

Irene held the doorknob in her hand.

The phone next to the receptionist's elbow started ringing.

The receptionist picked it up.

The senator for the interior, she said.

The way she pronounced *interior* sounded like stomach and guts to Irene.

The stations were on the other side of the Wall, under the other state.

Binoculars were glasses on the barren strip, good for nothing, not even for grass.

Governments, Irene thought, that last too long, longer than individuals can wait.

On the sunny afternoon the border guards were riding their bikes between watchtowers and barbed wire.

Irene said: A swallow skimming the walls.

Birch bushes surrounded the lilac.

And there was an unknown hand on Irene's skin when she touched her face. And the guts, Irene could almost see her guts. She carried them in her belly as in a pickling jar. And her heart and her tongue like deep frozen fruit.

Cut flowers, Irene thought. I'm going to buy myself cut flowers now.

Irene was startled when the older woman entered the flower shop, all wrapped in black. The doorbell began to ring as soon as the woman had set the first foot on the threshold.

Her face looked as if she were suffering as long as the fright was in it.

It put itself back together quickly, the face. First the eyes. Then the chin.

A cover for the burial of an urn, said the woman. Even the jugular didn't twitch anymore.

What flowers, the saleswoman asked.

Lilies are too heavy for me. Sometimes less is more.

The woman in black raised her eyebrows: But there must be regulations.

Cut flowers, said Irene.

I hope I can make up my own wreaths, said the saleswoman.

The woman in black dictated the address of the graveyard.

The funeral homes were always empty. There were houseplants in the windows. They were deep green. They were taken care of surreptitiously. In the background there was the scenery: marble stairs and marble columns. And coffins in between. Coffins with the thick iron rings of drain covers.

Irene hadn't seen a funeral yet in the city where she was living now. And sometimes she thought she would recognize cars transporting corpses on the highway. They were the white, long delivery cars without any lettering. They drove slowly. And there were the small, dark cars that were barely different from the others. Only the wheels, their wheels shimmered and threw a light behind themselves.

Ads for funeral homes were stuck on bus stops. They offered to transport corpses to their places of origin.

You could be buried in the earth, on sea, in the air. Or you could be cremated.

When Irene saw an airplane flying above the city and spreading a trail of white condensation in the sky, she knew the airplane was doing a burial in the sky.

Nobody on the street paid attention to it. Nobody raised his eyes. Nobody followed this dead one with his eyes.

When the trail of condensation disappeared Irene wondered:

In which country is the dead one falling now.

On the Nollendorferplatz Franz had called this country his homeland. He needed the state because of the city's refusal.

Abroad, said Franz, he had had to stand up for his homeland a few times.

Here, in the square, he was striving for the subtle difference that would isolate him from what homeland meant.

A state. And Franz, and in the midst of it all the perimeter of his ribs.

The blood at his temples was already cold.

But Irene couldn't help asking him this question:

Where do you carry your homeland if it's suddenly here against your will.

Franz didn't find a parking space on the street. He pulled at the wheel and cursed the city.

He cursed the city in which Irene lived and looked at Irene.

Irene felt for the first time that she liked this street and this day. And the day of tomorrow.

A city and a man, Irene thought.

Franz turned off the engine. The music too.

Irene thought, You can't stay here, and said:

The car can't stay here.

Irene got out. She looked over the roofs of the parked cars. She stood on the sidewalk. She wasn't thinking of a parking space. Because the sidewalk was empty, so empty that Irene felt the wind on her legs. And that the rustling of the bushes passed by her hands.

Franz slammed the car door.

Irene saw again that Franz had too many gestures that never ever changed. As with old people, they were dogged gestures, forever fixed. They had hardened and they made him old.

Franz was ten years younger than Irene. But his outer movements were so exact that they exceeded everything he did.

They were like gestures flung down. They were launched in such a short time with such ghostly precision that they stopped like details in front of your eyes. And they stopped because they were complete. Each gesture separated from the others. That's what made Franz older than Irene.

Complete down to the smallest gesture, Irene thought, and so confident that at twenty-five he stands with both feet on the ground of his life.

Franz was looking for a parking space in the side street.

Irene opened the glove compartment:

In his best years, she thought.

There was a tampon between a rag and a glove. It didn't belong to Irene.

She closed the compartment.

I'm shortening his life, she thought, if I think about it one more time, if I place him in the middle of his life.

It's my sister's, it's not what you think, said Franz.

What did she mean between his gestures, the wheel, the rattling keys.

Come, she said. I believe you.

Irene felt Franz's look like a stab in her face.

If you could see yourself, he said.

Irene talked through the courtyard, through the stairwell, through the room:

I imagined, before I came here, I'd often imagine the distance between you and me from the other country. There had been many distances. A different one every day. And all of them were right. They were right even after I landed because Stefan was at the airport. They stopped being right only when I saw your face weeks later. I had left by myself and I wanted to arrive together. Everything was the other way around. We were two when we left. But I arrived alone. I constantly write postcards to you. Postcards filled with writing. And I was empty. The coincidence that would put us at risk doesn't exist.

Franz put a pair of shoes in his suitcase. He laid a shirt above them. Then a jacket.

Franz's leaving was like a shrinking. As if he had longed for something that was destroying him.

There was almost no time between arriving, unpacking, packing, leaving.

Irene wrote a postcard: Franz, everything is invented when I relate to you. I could organize my life as if it had been entirely invented. But all these stories, how can you keep them alive.

Irene had brought along a different picture of Franz from her last trip to Marburg. His look had been absentminded and scattered over all streets at the same time. His gestures weren't old. They were fake. They were wrong.

Before Irene left, Franz had tried one more time to lay siege to the pavement between the railway station and the taxi stand. Without success.

Irene went downtown after Franz had left. Irene went to a store.

The light in the fitting room was brighter than the one in the store.

The man held the curtain open a crack:

Adele, the skirt is dark blue.

The saleswoman said it was black. The woman looked into the mirror.

So you trust her. Then I must be blind.

The woman slipped her hand under the skirt. She looked at the material on the back of her hand:

You've been wanting to fight with me ever since last night.

Fight. I could kill you, said the man.

Irene saw the woman putting on her boots in the strip between the curtain and the floor.

sixteen

I SAW YOU YESTERDAY IN THE STORE, SAID IRENE,
I saw you ten years from now.

Thomas's lips twitched.

Yesterday ten years from now.

Yesterday from yesterday. And today from today. And tomorrow from tomorrow in ten years. Individual days don't count if you're talking about ten years.

What did he look like.

Irene looked into Thomas's face as if she were putting skin on skin.

Thomas's larynx twitched.

His face was a little wider, said Irene. No wrinkles, but the spots where the wrinkles will be some day. The larynx harder and faster. Hands like yours. The roots of your nails sunken in the flesh a bit. A little more than yours.

Did you still like me.

I don't know, said Irene. It wasn't about you. It wasn't about him. It was about the resemblance.

Thomas looked at the roots of his nails.

I don't want to look like anyone.

He looked like you.

He is older, so I look like him.

I don't know him.

My mother had a woman friend when I was still a child. She had a son too. He was older than I am. But I was bigger than I should have been for my age. We seemed to be the same age. For years we had to dress the same: the same shoes, the same pants, the same shirts, the same sport caps. The same socks on Sundays. We had to hold hands in the street. We had to look like twins. That was the only way the two friends could take pleasure in us. We had to go to school together and we had to come home together after school. We were never friends. Later I avoided him. I hated him. I think it's because of him that later I loved a woman for a couple of years.

Thomas let coins fall into a peaked cap without bending over.

They are done for, said Thomas. They don't have a concept.

Irene only looked at the walking shoes.

Can you imagine that, said Thomas, can you imagine life without a concept.

In every place there was someone living on the edge. Someone who belonged to the city. Who had lost the naïveté. Who was not in a hurry.

That was not pity. It was a mild nausea. And fear. Only the thought that one day she could live on the edge and belong to the city made Irene inaccessible.

Irene's look was cold. She saw the same cold in Thomas's look. There had been a coldness in his thinking and a melancholy in his speech.

Irene tried to resist a child's look in the subway.

Thomas tore up a ticket. The ticket for this trip. Thomas didn't tear up the ticket absentmindedly. He was thinking about what he was doing. He was destroying the ticket, he tore up the small pieces into even smaller pieces.

He wasn't wrong, Irene thought, if he had the feeling that I see through him. I see through him to protect myself.

Thomas put his hand on Irene's knee. The hand was warm. Irene moved her foot so she could keep his hand on her knee.

I know of many who don't have a concept, said Thomas. It started with one. I wanted to help him. I took him home. Then he found out that I was gay and he got it all wrong.

And there was no reason, asked Irene.

I wanted to sleep with him. He took off in the middle of the night. I asked him. I didn't force him.

Thomas scattered the torn ticket on the ground:

I can't put an end to my unhappiness. I can only take it to others, said Thomas.

I understood, said Irene, why people were unhappy in the other country. The reasons were obvious. It hurt a lot to see the reasons day in day out.

A car parked so close and quiet next to Irene as if it wanted to get on the hem of her skirt. Thomas pulled Irene by her hand.

Come, it's green.

And here, said Irene. I know there are reasons. I can't see them. It hurts not to be able to see the reasons day in day out.

Look at me, said Thomas in front of a store window.

Irene looked over his hair instead of looking into his face.

You can also see reasons if you look at me. Reasons and consequences. I don't see anything.

A mail van stopped. A man held a bag full of letters up to the mail van. He pushed the door shut. Irene was leaning against Thomas's arm. His larynx twitched. Thomas was laughing. The car was humming.

The fifth shoe is now where your shoe stood before, said Irene.

Thomas lifted his foot. He looked at the sole:

This is one of the reasons.

He knocked on the sole with his fingertip.

I don't believe what I see, said Irene.

Irene pointed at a bunch of flowers. It was rigid and white.

You told me once to show you gillyflowers in the city. There are also violet ones.

The salesman smiled:

It's larkspur, it comes in violet too.

He pointed at another bunch.

I recognize the violet one, said Irene, but not the white one.

The white one, please, said Thomas. Without paper.

He held the bunch under Irene's chin.

Did you hear, it's larkspur.

You said you don't believe what you see.

Irene smelled the flowers:

They don't smell.

Thomas followed a young man with his eyes. Then the dog running behind the man. Or the man still, through the dog running behind him.

Irene was holding the flowers upside down. The tops of the larkspur were touching the sidewalk.

Thomas pressed Irene's face against his coat.

Irene took a strand of hair between her thumb and her index finger when Thomas bowed his head. Irene pulled the strand along her mouth. She opened her lips.

From one corner of her mouth to the other she noticed how Thomas's hair became thinner and thinner between her lips. Until it disappeared.

I know the kings of the East, said Irene. I'm afraid. And you're afraid you don't know them.

Sometimes, said Thomas, I know them too when you speak and use your hands to show me what you are saying.

Maybe they are the kings of the West then when I talk about the kings of the East here.

Irene put her fingertips on her mouth.

Thomas was keeping time with his knee:

Is there any difference.

Irene's fingertips smelled of larkspur.

Maybe, said Irene, because our wishes are always different.

Mine and yours, asked Thomas.

No, mine and mine. Our own wishes: We would like to drown when we are about to choke. And we would like to sweat when we are freezing.

Thomas raised his eyes.

Sometimes you could think we don't have brains. And don't even need any. Only the sensual force to live. Do you know where you realize it: on windy streets, on platforms outside, and on bridges. People move there so light and shameless that they almost touch the sky.

Sometimes I can see that the people passing by me are doing well, Irene said. They don't have a goal, only sensual steps driving them through the streets. Steps translate into other steps. Air hits across my face. I feel as if the leaves of all trees are rushing between my thighs. I become unsure. Who knows what will become of me when I'll do well.

I feel best, said Thomas, when I have money and I'm alone. Then I can go out on the streets without thinking about myself. I don't feel myself. I could laugh for no reason. I try on shirts, shoes, scarves until I don't have the power to put on clothes anymore. Sometimes I mistake myself for people going in another direction.

I take a shirt to the cash register when I get tired. It's always a shirt, always something out of the order between shoes and scarves. I want to buy myself shoes and I end up paying for a shirt.

It's uncanny how I can turn my eyes left and right unnoticed and see the dust on the shelves. And the threads hanging from the clothes all over. Black threads on white clothes, red threads on green clothes. And loose buttons.

I only try on a shirt to tear off loose buttons. I put the buttons in the pockets of other shirts hanging next to them. I drop them in a traveling bag. Or in a shoe.

For a long time I look for the shirt I try on when I feel I'm getting tired. The collar can't be squashed. The buttons can't be loose. And there can't be any thread hanging from it.

The bag crackles on the street. I walk lightly. I feel impatient, I want to be home standing alone in front of the mirror. I enter the apartment, I turn on the light. I tear off the clothes from my body and let them fall to the floor. I tremble when I put on the shirt. I look at my face in the mirror. Then I can only see the shirt.

The shirt is the only thing that counts in my apartment. It stands out from everything that's in the apartment.

I look at my face and it's like looking at it for the first time: I have the face of the man I would like to be. I like me. I feel my member. I go to the bathroom and I pant to myself, as a man pants to another man. I kiss what you can kiss of yourself. I love myself as a stranger would love me.

I need a night to pass over the shirt. I hang it on the back of the chair so I can see it from my bed. So I can see it whenever I turn on the light. I might even wake up because I want to see the shirt.

Unfortunately, I never wake up when a new shirt is hanging in my room. I'm tired of shopping. I sleep like a log. In the morning it's over. The shirt is like all the other shirts. Like all the objects in my house. It doesn't count anymore. It doesn't stand out anymore.

I put on the shirt. I only look in the mirror when I have it on. I have the face of a man I don't want to be.

I have a feeling like somebody borrowed me the day before and returned me during the night, when I was asleep, said Thomas.

How often do you do it, asked Irene.

Ask the social workers, said Thomas, once a month.

Once a month, that's enough, said Irene.

What do you think of me now, said Thomas.

Look at me if you are disgusted with me.

seventeen

THE CONDUCTOR OPENED THE DOOR OF THE
compartment. The younger of the two men took his ticket and
his ID from his coat pocket without being asked to do so.

The conductor punched the three ladies' tickets and the
older man's ticket.

The younger man looked at his ID photo for a long time,
reading his parents' names, his place of birth, and the date he
was born.

The conductor held out his hand for his ticket. The man
hadn't finished reading yet. He was startled when the conductor pulled the ticket out of his hand.

The ID fell on the floor. The man's look was so distressed,
as if by reading his ID the man had realized for the first time
how long he had already lived.

The man's confusion was so great after the conductor had
closed the compartment door that he began talking to the
older man as if he were in the middle of a discussion. He kept
talking, so absorbed by what he said that his whole body was
involved. He couldn't draw his breath. His words got caught in
his throat and tears ran down his face. He didn't wait for any
approval or contradiction.

He pronounced his father's name and his mother's name in such a way as if the information on his ID forced him to tell his whole life story.

They all got off at a small railway station.

Irene wasn't sure if she was going to Marburg anymore. She took the ticket out of her purse. The name of the city didn't give her a sense of security. It wasn't a destination.

The meaning of the trip was like cold fingertips. It was where the body ends. Irene didn't feel it. The meaning of the trip was connected with effort. It also had to do with Franz.

The land behind the window of the train was flat. But Irene could see that the plain was elevated. A plateau. The fields couldn't stand the fir and the fir couldn't stand the fields here.

The village passing by stood in a fog.

Nobody was walking on the streets.

A man was standing on the roof of his house at the end of the village. He climbed into the chimney.

The stadium was far from the village. It was so close to the forests that you had to feel the wood when running.

In the empty stadium, headlights burning by themselves were casting light on the grass.

When the train stopped Irene looked at the railway station's clock. It said Paradeplatz on the dial.

A woman got on.

After the train had pulled out, Irene saw that the woman sat with her back to the direction in which the train was going. The seat opposite her was not taken. Irene thought, The woman could take that seat now. Irene expected her to.

Irene looked at the woman because she didn't: Her knee, her fingers, they were resting on her thighs. Her skirt, her blouse. Her earlobes, her chin.

When Irene got to the cheeks the woman had fallen asleep. She breathed more slowly than Irene. And evenly.

Irene was angry because the woman could breathe so slowly and evenly. Because the picture Irene made of her didn't bother her. Because she didn't want to correct that picture.

When Irene got off she knew the woman would travel much farther. She was turning her back on the whole world by sitting and sleeping the way she did.

Looking at everything she saw, Irene had to ask herself if she could live in this city.

Irene imagined the city without people. She felt the closeness of water and a mountain. That closeness was cool. It was not meant as flight. It was a closeness that you should not step into.

Not only Marburg became stranger and stranger, but other cities too, the more often Irene visited them. People close to her were living in those cities.

Irene had the feeling that by looking at these towns she removed the people close to her from them. She tried hard not to show how strange she felt.

But the people close to Irene let no occasion slip by to show how close they felt to these towns.

They knew precisely what they were supposed to do in every place. They were shopping very fast. They ordered coffee at once. They touched store windows, walls, and fences when passing by. They would tear leaves from the first bush in a park. They would even put a leaf in their mouths. They would let stones fall into the water from bridges. They would sit down on the first bench in squares. They didn't look around. They started speaking immediately.

They knew how to skillfully avoid passersby on large streets swarming with people. Irene stayed a step behind them.

Then Irene saw that the people close to her carried the city they were living in on their backs.

In moments like these Irene realized her life had run down to observations. Observations rendered her unable to act.

The actions Irene forced herself to undertake weren't actions. They got stuck in their beginnings. They were beginnings that fell apart. Not even individual gestures would remain complete.

Consequently, Irene lived not in the things but in their consequences.

Irene walked the paths she had walked with Franz or the others, alone this time.

She needed pretexts and excuses to do this.

Sometimes she even had to lie.

There were asters on the large streets where you can see so far out that it looked as if the cars were driving through the trees for a while as if they had been sprayed. The asters rustled and were heavy. They smelled of salt and water.

Every time Irene walked by asters alone she thought: One should have a vase or a grave in this city.

Irene didn't tell the people close to her about this.

She only told them that there were asters on the large streets where you could see so far out that it seemed as if the cars were driving through the trees for a while.

And every time she said this, the people close to her were moved.

It wasn't because of the streets, the cars, the trees, and the flowers. Just the connections.

They had integrated so callously that the connection tortured them. It penetrated them like a pointed object. They became so helpless that Irene would have liked to disappear behind what she had just said.

If this happened on the first day, and if Irene stayed on for another couple of days, all the days were just a continuous farewell.

There was a monument in the square. The taxi driver was reading the newspaper. Irene got in. Irene got out again:

No, she didn't want to see Franz.

The naked woman stood in the water. There were benches around the water. The sun fell from one direction. So the water of the fountain was half in the sun and half in the shade.

Nobody moved in the square. Men were sitting on the benches in the sun. They were rubbing bread to pieces on the stone edge of the fountain.

The men weren't talking to each other. They didn't look at each other. They were all doing the same thing: for hours they had been rubbing bread to pieces on the stone edge.

It was agonizing that the men had been rubbing bread for so long. Because there were gray birds up on the monument. They weren't bigger than fingers. They were trembling with impatience.

The water was totally dark when the sun moved behind a high building.

The men wiped the bread crumbs from the benches. They stood up and brushed their clothes. They left. They walked away one after the other as if they wanted to leave each other time to disappear.

When the last one had gone the square was so quiet as if no one had been here. As if the bread were growing out of the stone edge. Then the birds came in flocks. They ate, they sipped water, they flew away. They landed on the monument. They looked. They came back again.

Irene recognized one of the birds. It had already eaten

three times. It had a bald spot on its thigh. On this spot its skin was as gray as its feathers. Its thigh wasn't bigger than a cricket's leg.

The light sank and was heavy.

The birds remained light. In a few moments they ate more than the size of their bodies.

The water splashed.

Irene felt old on the outside and powerless on the inside.

The pavement was oblique. Irene walked as if she were a pile of stones that pulled itself up and threw itself together.

She talked herself into things that could not be. And she talked herself out of things that could not disappear. She tried to talk herself out of them. Franz belonged to these things. Yes, to these things. Because people you can handle. And Irene couldn't handle Franz.

For a moment Irene let Franz disappear. But then, with the edge of a thought, she had to think of Franz again. She only had to touch on his name and here was the powerlessness again.

Irene blamed the other country for it. The sea, the railway tracks, and the drawing on the sand with the small stone for Marburg. The effusiveness of her wishes interfered with the shabbiness of the things outside. Things that were never allowed to meet were one and the same in the other country.

So were Irene and Franz. And this loose summer.

Irene felt she had been deceived for years. Provoked and cheated.

Waiting, Franz had said on his last visit, what do you mean by it.

I knew you would come sometime. So I've been waiting.

Did you want more. You obviously wanted more, Franz had said. You wanted longing because you had your own. Now you are here. And I'm here in this room. And your longing is the same as if you weren't here and I weren't here.

You have a childlike longing, Franz had said, wishes that don't know what they mean.

Irene had become bitter. She couldn't let herself go when she was with Franz.

Irene knew so precisely what happened when she was with Franz, as if she were sewing a dress out of her skin. What happened. What didn't happen.

The small connections between skin and skin weren't made.

If anything could pull Irene along it was a cogwheel. A machine off track that kept pounding.

Every time Irene bought a postcard she imagined Franz's face.

Irene didn't buy the postcards that didn't allow Franz's face, that drove it out when it was already there.

What Irene would write on the back of the postcards determined itself.

Choosing the postcards was left to Irene. Through Franz.

Many places in the city were occupied by Franz. Irene had thought of Franz in those places. When she set foot in those places again she realized she had thought of him there.

That's why Irene couldn't write postcards in those places without writing the same thing. And Irene didn't want to write to Franz what she had already written to him.

The places occupied mixed themselves so intimately into her thoughts that there wasn't any free space left for new thoughts.

Irene had to avoid these places on her walks through the city, she had to avoid them until a new season came.

Then the places would become unfamiliar again. Or not

known anymore. They would keep their distance from Irene's thoughts. New coincidences appeared. Franz had withdrawn from those places again.

There was a coming and going of places cleared and occupied. This connected Irene to Franz while also separating her from him. This was a connection between Irene and the city.

But it was laborious, this connection, often so scattered between the city and her skull that Irene had to invent it.

The places occupied by Franz were packed with camouflaged things that would suddenly emerge.

Detours, Irene thought, Franz uses detours to appear and to disappear.

It was torment to Irene that she couldn't see Franz's face as he was reading the postcards. This was the biggest disadvantage to distances for Irene.

And the city where Franz lived drifted farther and farther away in its own streets. And in the evening it fell into the courtyard. Or was it the elder bush that pulled its leaves like ears closer to its branches because the light vanished.

Marburg was so far away that the name was the only thing left. The name was smaller than Frankfurt on the map. The city was as big as Irene's fingernail.

Irene covered the letters with her fingertip so she could hold on to them.

There were more ways Marburg had found to drift away than Irene had trucks in her head.

Marburg drifted away even through Irene's fingertip. Even through Irene's shoes as she walked.

Every day Irene gave the city Franz lived in the chance to drift away. Because Irene could only move in one direction, the city Franz lived in moved away in the other direction.

Marburg looked for the outermost point of all its streets to remove itself.

The city Franz lived in lay under yellow leaves with long, reddish stems whenever Irene found it in her thoughts.

Irene saw an airplane landing on TV. It was late, the news announcer said.

Irene couldn't see the lateness on the screen.

Just the snow that supposedly was the reason for the late arrival, as the announcer said.

In Moscow there was snow on the ground already.

The man coming out of the airplane was both a pilot and an official guest of the state.

The sky had a bright half and a dark half. Military music was playing.

When the pilot and official guest stepped on the snow in his dark suit, he was bigger and wider than in all other contexts Irene remembered.

Maybe the sky had a bright half and a dark half; maybe it was because the snow was so white and the suit so dark that Irene said:

Each landing is an attack on the city.

Irene said the sentence out loud as the official guest saluted.

eighteen

THE OLD MAN TOTTERED INTO IRENE'S APART-
ment. He closed the door behind him with his fingers spread.
Irene saw the dirt under the edges of his nails.

His hair was gray and dry as with old people who don't
lose hair. It had become thicker now since this lifeless, growing
color was all that was left in it. It grew to the detriment of the
face. It hung down to his shoulders.

The water was running in the bathtub over the skin-col-
ored pantyhose. They were swelling. Foam welled up at their
edges.

The old man looked into the bathtub.

Like floating corpses.

Irene dried her dripping hands:

Where did you come from.

From Nollendorfplatz.

Where is your peaked cap.

In the subway.

Where is it going.

To Krumme Lanke.

What is it doing there. Who is going to help it to change
trains.

Yeah right, what is it doing there.

And tomorrow, what are you going to do tomorrow.

We'll see.

Nobody will give you money without your cap.

Maybe it'll come back.

The man saw the collage on the kitchen wall. He pointed to the open gate in front of which the pavement led into emptiness:

I know that street well. Every stone. And how the dust swirls. The wind also blows on windless days. The pavement leads out of the gate. On your picture it leads into the gate. In your picture the direction is wrong.

Who sent you here.

Thomas. Your picture is empty, Irene. Not only empty, but also dead.

You mean, because you always sit there and you are not in the picture.

I would be like the picture if I were in it.

The man looked at the kitchen table:

You gave me ten marks once. I didn't let the money lie in the cap. I reached for the money and you looked at me. I've known you since then. The wind was blowing.

That was a year ago.

Half a year. You haven't given me anything since then. Why didn't you give me the money in installments.

I avoided you. I often thought of you. But thoughts don't buy money.

Irene pointed at the collage. Standing on tiptoe she pointed at a picture:

Can you see those petty criminals standing by the water. They wear peaked caps like yours. They flee the cities. Thomas said they are lonely if there isn't any mischief to do. You see, they are in the picture and they aren't dead.

They are young. That will change once they are as old as I
am.

If they live as long.

Irene would have liked to count her months in this country on the hands of the petty criminals. She would have liked
to say the numbers out loud, insistent, at their thin, imperti-
nent fingers often injured by hard objects. There would have
been false numbers and mischief in the offing.

Until their return to the cities, Irene would have liked to
consider these helpless fingers as her own hands on the kitchen
table.

The man listened:

Don't forget the floating corpses, they are swimming
toward us. Look, I'm wearing a Berlin coat. Do you see the
buttons.

The man was wearing a trench coat with three huge buttons.

You think your cap will come back. Do you want me to
give you one.

The man smiled:

I don't take any objects, I only take money.

Irene picked up an apple from the fruit tray. She pulled
out a bill and put the apple back.

You had hidden the money. From whom.

From me. I thought I would forget about it. I wanted to
save some. Irene put the bill in front of the man's hand on the
kitchen table.

The man raised his index finger and moved it the way you
shake your head:

I only take money on the street.

The trench coat's buttons had a silver edge. Raised high.

And the buttons were deep. They were deeper than Irene's coffee cups.

You can sleep here tonight, said Irene.

When it rang for the second time she stood next to the phone. She let it ring four times, then she picked it up.

Hey, said Stefan, I'm in town again. I have often thought of you in Ramallah, of your sentence that even the air has eyes when everything is under surveillance.

Have you been shadowed, asked Irene.

Watched. I carried my files and the soldiers their guns. Six of one, half a dozen of the other. People were afraid to talk to me.

And secretly.

Sometimes. It would have worked more often if I hadn't been so blond.

You could have dyed your hair.

What about the face and the eyes, said Stefan.

Irene saw the quiet scaffold in the courtyard.

I brought something along. We can compare, said Stefan.

A rubber bullet.

The iron has become thicker and the rubber even thinner. Now that's a hard egg to crack, you'll see.

You want to show me a bullet and you're talking about eggs.

You are so meticulous, you analyze each word. How come you analyze each word. How is Thomas.

When he wonders about it he opens the closet door and looks into the mirror. Do you want to see him.

No.

That's what he says too. Then he asks about you. Am I playing a role.

But you aren't a beggar, or do they blackmail you too. Don't let anybody put you off. It goes like this, said Stefan: A woman meets a student at the seashore. The student has a sister. She had been the girlfriend of a sociologist years ago, and she still sees him sometimes. One day she calls him and sends him to the airport instead of her brother. She says: The woman from the sea is coming.

The old man waved.

The apartment door closed behind him.

This is how the sociologist met the woman from the sea. Stefan laughed:

And as it usually goes, the sociologist knows a bookstore owner who breaks up with an actor in late summer. The student and the woman from the sea, that's like rare closeness and frequent distance. And the bookstore owner is lonely. And the woman from the sea is foreign. And the sociologist is often away. And as it usually happens, the bookstore owner leapfrogs the sociologist.

Irene didn't say anything.

Have I really not said anything wrong, or do you sometimes turn a blind eye, Stefan asked.

When you are malicious, and when you're sad, and when you talk about women, you speak in such a way that I don't need to do it.

I'm going to get my hair done now, the trip messed me up.

So I hear.

You'll see me tonight.

Don't forget the rubber bullets.

I want to see you and you want to compare, said Stefan.

The money was on the kitchen table, and the beggar had taken three apples.

Stefan read the menu out loud:

Sea devil.

What is sea devil, Irene asked.

An animal.

I haven't thought of sea anemone.

An animal from the sea.

Nothing from the sea.

Rainbow trout, said Stefan.

No.

From the mountains in the rivers.

I know. I haven't thought of dragonflies.

Tastes good.

For a while.

Tonight.

For years. Those are gone.

What do you have against trout.

The other country.

What does that have to do with fish.

You don't have to think of me when you eat fish, said Irene.

But I want to.

You don't know that, said Irene.

A rubber bullet lay between Irene's hand and the plate.

Eat a slice of bread and the fish will taste better, said Stefan.

Women who eat much bread get children, said Irene.

Why is it that you can't handle children at all, Stefan asked.

Irene said without thinking: They are eerie because they are still growing.

It was only after this sentence that Irene wondered how

Stefan knew she couldn't handle children. It was only after this sentence was out that Irene realized how much she would have liked to have hidden it.

Stefan laughed without making a sound.

A red vein crawled from Stefan's eyeball onto the bridge of his nose.

I get scared when they're playing, said Irene.

The light in the restaurant was dim. Smoke gathered under the lampshades.

Everybody pretends to love children, said Irene.

Stefan raised the glass to his mouth:

Were you ever a child. I'm not sure anymore when I look at you.

Irene looked through the windowpane. Noises came through from the streets: the trickling, the scraping, and the bustling.

I was a child, said Irene. Not beautiful and not good. I was loved. I only had to play and to grow. I didn't have to change.

I think it's going to rain, said Stefan.

Or somebody is throwing sand, said Irene, it's late. I was beaten out of love.

Irene knew that her fear for children had become bigger. Bigger since she had been living here.

A child was seldom alone on the street.

Children ran after each other in groups of three or five. They put their bikes upside down when they were among themselves. When strangers came near, they banged on mailboxes or whipped the walls and the street with dry branches.

The noises hurt. Irene felt sorry for the bikes, the mailboxes, and the dry branches, that's how she felt.

Irene avoided the children. She crossed the streets in unpermitted places so as not to have to meet them.

The children noticed Irene's fear. They shouted after her. Most of the time Irene didn't understand what they were shouting. But the tone was superior. That Irene understood.

On a Sunday afternoon the street was empty like a church. Children were playing in front of a gate. Irene couldn't get out of their way and she felt as if she were entering a forbidden place. The children were playing like dumb figures.

Irene walked fast. She felt her cheeks getting hot.

Whore, the boy said. Two girls lifted their dolls in front of their faces and laughed.

Irene stopped. She saw silk panties under the dolls' skirts.

Better a whore than a fascist, said Irene startling herself. The boy was no older than five. He repeated the word: fascist.

That night, on her pillow, in the space between her forehead and her mouth, Irene brought people together who didn't know each other. The worker Irene had picked, Franz, Thomas, and Stefan were sitting at a table in a seafood restaurant.

Pictures in black frames were hanging on the walls. Many frames and far too many illustrations in one frame. They were sea animals, black and white, so tightly put together as if they had been let loose against each other with jagged scissors and feathered pincers.

You'll notice that some are dead and some alive when you look at them for a long time, said Franz when Irene entered the seafood restaurant.

There was a smell of gillyflowers and fish in the room.

When Irene sat down at the table, she noticed a woman sitting there who looked like her. She had the same features. But the face as a whole had a strange expression. She was the other Irene. She had a deep voice. She was eating tunafish salad.

When I was a child, said the other Irene in her deep voice, I always heard that love was red, faith was blue, and jealousy was yellow. Back then I could understand the world.

And hope green, said the worker.

Hope is green in swarms, said Franz. Who said that.

He looked at Irene.

I don't know.

I did.

The worker laughed.

The vinegar wilted the lettuce leaves.

What stops us from going on with this, Stefan asked.

The other Irene touched the worker's belly:

The years, nothing but the years.

The worker kissed her hand:

A man without a belly is a cripple, madam.

Irene was sitting between Thomas and Franz. She was drinking apple juice. To me traveling still means freezing, she said. Oh, this summer freeze. As soon as I left the railway station I noticed the asphalt running through my toes. All the shoes with leather roses. The women's naked armpits in which the city pulls itself together. I know it's only my imagination, swindling me.

Take a look at this, Stefan called, this barkeeper, this short, quick barkeeper is a Palestinian.

The worker kissed the other Irene on the mouth. He said with wet lips:

When grandfather took grandmother nobody knew about Misses and Ladies.

The worker looked at Irene:

And men in swimsuits walking out of the sun into churches. There should be a law against that.

Yes, it's all a big swindle, said Stefan to Irene, why do you believe these things. They are all made up and you believe in them.

Yes, Irene smiled, I feel like beginning my life with a crime when nobody you love is there and the cities are so muddled.

Irene looked at Thomas. Then at Franz. One had taken the other's face.

I'm going to get myself some strawberry ice cream, said Franz with Thomas's mouth.

The other Irene stood up from the chair:

I think I'm hot. I can't look at the sea animals in the pictures anymore.

These are gillyflowers, said Stefan, I'm almost drunk with gillyflowers.

The other Irene's voice became even deeper:

Well, I'm going if there is nothing else to talk about. We could phone tomorrow. Who wakes me up tomorrow. I never pick up when it rings. But when I'm sleeping I'm curious. I can't control myself. Once I know who it is I'd like to hang up again.

The worker looked at Irene. Then at the other Irene:

Which one of you two is the dummy.

Thomas or Franz walked Irene home. Irene looked into the moon that was behind a tree. Then at the tree's shadow hanging above the house door. Between the moon and the shadow, the face Irene kissed had a bluish color. Not even after the long French kiss did Irene know whether Thomas or Franz had kissed her.

One of the two said:

When you kiss you are not allowed to look at the moon, at shadows and at trees. You should only have eyes for me.

That's tiring, said Irene. The two of you should never leave me.

And one of the two said:
Not you. If it has to be the other Irene.

nineteen

TWO LETTERS FELL OUT OF THE MAILBOX. IRENE took the one, she recognized the gray, rough envelope, in her hand without examining it.

Irene thought of Dana and tore open the second letter. Irene read walking up the stairs: The letterhead said Senate for the Interior. It said underneath: You have received German citizenship. In a week Irene was supposed to report to room 304 to be invested with German citizenship.

Irene wasn't excited. She read on as if the notification weren't about her. Irene didn't understand the context in which the words *banquet* and *welcoming speech* appeared in the last paragraph.

Her stomach floated between her larynx and her knees. She sat down at the kitchen table to catch it. She didn't feel the chair, she looked down at herself to know if she was really sitting. She opened Dana's letter.

The drummer had hanged himself, Dana wrote.

The back of the chair pressed against her back.

The drummer was Irene's age.

Irene bent forward, she put her chin on the table.

Irene knew a time would come when the dead and the living would be equally divided. But back then Irene had thought this time would come later. It would come when you yourself don't have much longer to live.

There were some friends that were as old as Irene and dead. They had begun to look alike since they had died. A resemblance on the edge. But it was the same edge.

The living, always strangers, looked like the friends since they had died. Strangers in the city Irene lived in, and strangers in other cities. The living scared Irene. They carried the dead by her once more. They didn't know. They also didn't know why Irene's look rested on them for so long without mellowing.

No wonder, Dana wrote. The readiness to die for a small thing was big. His face had become too hot recently and he had plunged head first into every moment.

The man you can only see from behind is the main character in the collage.

Irene folded Dana's letter to the size of half a postcard and put it in her handbag without the envelope.

Irene noticed that she was in the middle of the city even though she was still standing in front of the house door.

A woman carried a living rose in her hair.

For three days Irene had seen people lacking the right or the left index finger on the streets everywhere. Since today, the third day, Irene felt that her index fingers were endangered. She tried not to use them.

When holding the door, the phone receiver, the cutlery, the cigarettes, and the key, Irene used her thumbs and her middle fingers. She stretched her index fingers away from the objects she touched. The objects didn't miss Irene's index fingers. They had changed. They acted as if Irene's index fingers were pointless. After a couple of days the index fingers bothered Irene. They had not only become unnecessary, they had also become uglier and older than the other fingers.

Now Irene wished her index fingers would disappear.

Irene saw the place at the Landwehrkanal where she had met Thomas.

Creepers scattered blossoms like flour. The water had the same reflection as then. A face was growing between decayed poles.

Irene didn't want to admit it: The wife of the dictator from the other country looked like Rosa Luxemburg.

There was a curse on Rosa Luxemburg's face. The dictator's wife had carried this face into old age long ago. She was a dictatoress.

In the evening she walked through the mansion at the dictator's side. She looked for a safe place to sleep in the many rooms. Servants carried beds through the doors past eavesdropping velvet.

The night became presumptuous in the mansion. The guard detachment and the dogs changed directions when the leaves shone with rain.

Poverty was asleep in the country.

A bird rustled in the branches. Red rose hips grew in the bushes. Irene walked to and fro at the bus stop.

Two women were sitting on the bench.

I've never contracted anything, said one of them, I boil my underwear.

Albert might think something has happened to me, said the other woman.

The bus went slowly. It let all cars go by. It was full of small faces. They rocked when the bus stopped.

A man kissed a much younger woman.

The street narrowed so the bus could barely get by the houses. A quiet thought out to the last detail was lying on the roofs. Nothing could overcome it, no wind and no engine. Least of all the small, dizzy faces. They were silent. The silence had not been thought out.

The silence in the driving bus made a fool of itself in front of the quiet lying on the roofs, thought out to the last detail.

The pedestrian precinct was swarming with heads, bags, and shoes.

In the afternoon an unexpected time suddenly fell out of the middle of the sky. It was closing time.

The pedestrians left the street so quickly, as if they thought it would swallow the ones who stayed past closing time.

Water stripes crawled under closed store doors. Saleswomen were still slipping around the corners.

Then the pedestrian precinct was empty. The sun twitched. The water stripes didn't go far.

A man came out of a side street. He carried a rolled-up towel under his arm. He asked Irene about the public bath. He was a foreigner. His voice was so unsure, as if he had traveled inadvertently to an uninhabited city.

Irene saw the towel, the beach sandals. She couldn't open her mouth. He was gone already.

There was a store window where he had stood. Goggle-eyed gold with bloody rubies was shining in the sun in small boxes.

Irene thought there had to be broken pieces, furniture, and glass because the street rose after this light, above the roofs.

Irene crossed the street on red. She ran very close to the hoods of the oncoming cars. She was breathing fast. She had the feeling that she both risked her life and saved it.

Neither dead nor alive, Irene thought. It was almost joy. On some days Irene left the house as if ready for an accident.

As soon as she walked through the courtyard she already knew she would play with the red light outside, on the streets.

A lethargy began to develop in Irene because she knew this. It was sleepy and vigilant at the same time.

Irene noticed that her body was programmed to live a long life. So she wanted to push herself into a corner where life wasn't sure anymore.

She surprised herself by being prepared for the worst and not able to deal with the unforeseeable, smallest things.

You know, Irene wrote, every morning I wake up with the certainty that I do something wrong. If I didn't have this certainty I'd remain in bed looking at the ceiling and waiting. If the morning were a talk, an orange, or a newspaper, I could use it. Then I go out. People were tortured in the most beautiful houses. I can't be happy those houses are there. The German widows have square faces and frizzy hair like snow and steel.

Rabbits live in the holes in the ground by the Wall. They scare me more than the guns. They are dead people metamorphosed. Field brown. You can only see them when they run. Then their eyes are bigger than their bellies. Since I've been living here the detail has been bigger than the whole. It doesn't bother me. It bothers the things, they don't like showing it.

Irene's hand was limp when she wanted to write Franz's address on the postcard.

She wrote down Thomas's address.

When Irene walked through the courtyard the worker she had picked wasn't on the scaffold. He stood in the glass next to the wall. Irene saw his face. Pear skin with small, black dots. Very ripe pears. And his eyes were green. Or were they elder bush leaves with cheeks underneath and temples next to them. And a restlessness coming out of the eyeball and taking itself back inside.

The concrete machine was turning.

You live alone, said the worker.

How come.

You stand at the window. You come and go alone.

But you come alone too, said Irene.

I come to work.

You never stand at the window.

Only for a while when I air out.

He pointed at the scaffold:

They made a bet that you'd stand at the window in a moment. They bet on it every day.

And.

And you stand at the window every day. And you stand at the window as on cue when they have made their bet.

You're watching me, said Irene.

And you're watching us.

How much work do you still have to do.

You can see that if you stand at the window.

The worker reached into his jacket pocket. He turned on the red radio.

The mortar drum was turning.

Classical music came from the worker's pocket.

There was a man with a traveling bag here once.

And he left soon after, said Irene.

I know, the worker said.

At eight minutes after two P.M.

In the morning a feather lay in the bathroom. It was light gray and light.

It must have been covered by the darker feathers in the wing, Irene thought.

She pressed toothpaste out of the tube. She put the toothbrush on the edge of the sink.

Irene picked up the feather. She looked at the bottom of

the bathtub. A pubic hair whirling in the running water. A hair from her head was stuck at the edge. The pubic hair and the hair from her head in the tub. The feather between her thumb and index finger.

Irene passed the feather across her throat. It was soft. The words *pigeon murderer* came to Irene's mind.

She wrote *pigeon murderer* on a postcard. She put the postcard and the feather into an envelope. She wrote her own address on the envelope.

Irene got into the bath when she came back from the mailbox. The toothpaste and the toothbrush on the edge of the sink worried her.

When Irene came in that afternoon, there was a feather in the room, next to the flower vase.

The feather was darker and harder than the feather in the bath. Irene put it on the desk.

That evening the building manager said in the stairwell:

You should close your window when you go out.

Before she went to bed Irene put the feather in the closet between her clothes.

After the phone had rung five times, Irene saw the receiver in her hand as if from afar.

Irene felt caught by Stefan's voice. It asked:

What are you doing.

And the voice was closer than Irene's own mouth.

Nothing.

Why do you always come back to me in the evenings.

During the day you're talking, or you don't pick up. Or you pick up and hang up.

Do all men have to be gay, Stefan asked.

Irene swallowed:

Who said so.

Nobody. You make me pick up these ideas.

How come. You are wrong.

Stefan's voice became soft.

Not this time. Thomas is happy with you. Even after a withered apple.

Irene heard herself breathing. The numbers on the dial were shimmering.

Are you freezing, Stefan asked.

Irene hung up. Her eyes were so bitter they hurt her own face, they looked at the phone cord along the floor up to the spot where it crawled into the wall.

The lampshade's shadow on the table. The doorknob shining. The key's shadow at the door.

The clock was ticking. It was long past midnight. Irene couldn't distinguish anymore between the dials: the clock's and the phone's. Both were targets. All Irene could think of was a pigeon feather: light gray and lightly arched behind her forehead.

Irene saw the illuminated window in the courtyard. The woman without the blouse wasn't speaking. She was just sitting and looking.

There was coldness and stubbornness in the contact Irene's look made with the illuminated window. And a forced silence.

To evade the silence, Irene walked to the closet. She locked the closet with the key.

The desire to sleep was like an addiction.

And the desire to go far away. To look out of the compartment's window into the wake of the landscape that turned away in green schlieren and disappeared. And people in the compartment were getting on. People eating and sleeping. People who weren't giving anything away. That were getting off at big railway stations, standing undecided in the noise for a while. They were walking warily through the people waiting and into the cities.

They were walking so warily that long after they had disappeared you didn't know why they had stood there in the wind in their creased clothes. You could suspect or guess that they crossed squares, lost, with their bags under their arms. That they walked by store windows without looking inside. That they sat on wet benches as if stranded on the banks of unknown rivers. That they looked into the emptiness on stairs under memorials.

People who did not know anymore whether they were travelers in thin shoes in these cities. Or inhabitants with hand luggage.

Irene was lying in the dark thinking of the city.

Irene refused to think good-bye.